PALS
2.73

D1106567

UNIVERSITY OF WINNIPEG
DISCARDED
PORTAGE & BALMORAL
WINNIPEG 2. MAN.   CANADA

DISCARDED

THE KILLING GAME

By the same author

SNATCH OF MUSIC
TWO SETS TO MURDER
OUT BY THE RIVER
TWO AFTER MALIC
RIOT '71
DOUBLE-TAKE
FALL OF TERROR

THE KILLING GAME

by

LUDOVIC PETERS

PR
6031
·E7K5

HODDER AND STOUGHTON

*The characters in this book are entirely imaginary
and bear no relation to any living person*

Copyright © 1969 by Ludovic Peters

First printed 1969

SBN 340 04263 X

*All rights reserved. No part of this publication may be
reproduced or transmitted in any form or by any means,
electronic or mechanical, including photocopy, record-
ing, or any information storage and retrieval system,
without permission in writing from the publisher.*

*Printed in Great Britain for Hodder and Stoughton Limited,
St. Paul's House, Warwick Lane, E.C.4, by Northumberland
Press Limited, Gateshead*

PART ONE

*Be not forgetful to entertain
strangers: for thereby some have
entertained angels unawares.*
Hebrews 13:1

One of medium height, perhaps a little plump, his light-brown skin smooth, his eyes darker than his skin and soft as if anxious, a tentative smile twitching compressed lips, lifting a black moustache; the other tall, white-faced, brown hair falling as if uncared-for towards grey eyes, pale eyebrows gathered in a half-frown, broad mouth ready to fall open into some suitable and vigorous expression, the head pushed forward for aggression or hospitality. One outside the bright yellow door, the other within it, holding it with a broad hand, for the moment holding up all possibility of the other's entrance. Grey eyes stared into brown; brown eyes, smiling, pleaded. Elsewhere, London growled through a spring morning.

"I'm Martin Prescott."

Broad hand left the door, stretched, a little hesitantly, towards the smaller man, still watchful on the landing.

"I am Hassan Burani."

The hands met, clasped. Tall Martin Prescott began to laugh, nodding vigorously, his hair tumbling over his forehead, that broad, white, slightly-lined intellectual's forehead. He stood to one side, clapped Hassan Burani lightly on the left shoulder.

"Auspicious," he cried. "Important moment. After all, a sort of marriage."

Hassan Burani laughed too, his tight lips parting, small teeth glittering within them, charming yet curiously predatory, as if he might at some malicious, unexpected moment leap ferociously and bite.

"No more than an engagement as yet," he said. He spoke in a quick, clipped way, emphasising consonants, setting forth each word with precision.

"Oh, you'll like it," Martin Prescott insisted. "You're sure to like it. I decorated it myself—and it's got to be good. I'm an architect, after all . . ."

"Oh, that, all that—decoration, you know . . ." And Hassan Burani laughed politely, his small teeth white in the white hall

7

he stood in now, his skin smooth, dark, his hair black. Behind him, Martin Prescott smacked the door to, led him along a corridor, pointing swiftly left and right as he walked.

"The kitchen. My bedroom. Over there's the loo; bathroom's next to it and separate—useful, that, sometimes. Here's the sitting room—we'd share that, of course. That's a sort of workroom for me. Here it is, the one at the end . . ."

He threw a door open, his arm flinging wide in a sort of flourish. The room revealed was long, high, cool, all whites and greys and plain, varnished wood. Lime curtains swung slowly in a light breeze; beyond them, long branches fuzzy with the year's furled leaves criss-crossed the dappled sky.

"Well?"

Hassan Burani laughed again. "Oh, yes. I feel really almost inadequate . . ."

"Oh, if you eat and sleep and sometimes talk, you'll do. You'll do."

They walked back, quietly happy with each other. The engagement, they felt, would be short, the marriage happy.

"Well, and this is the sitting room . . ."

Hassan Burani nodded. "Yes. Beautiful."

Deep black couch, heavy armchairs, a brightness of rug and cushion; three paintings on the white walls, all big, two of them cool, one violent, this one adding the sudden fistful of colour the room might have been insipid without. A metal sculpture in the corner, one wall fat with books, outside the window a stabbing of chimney pots, a petrified storm of roofs.

"Rent went up," Martin Prescott said, "and rates. It's a flat I like. So I thought I'd share it.'

"It is a fine flat."

"You're a student?"

"Post-graduate. Social anthropology."

"Ah," Martin Prescott solemnly murmured, then shrugged, grinned.

Hassan Burani said, "Sometimes it is difficult for a . . . foreigner to find a place . . ."

"I know. But I'm not giving charity."

"I was only going to mention my gratitude."

"Don't. To yourself you may be ordinary; to anyone like me you're exotic. A sort of perambulating travel poster—I'll ask

8

you all sorts of damned silly questions about where you come from, customs, women, food . . . And that's in addition to your sharing the rent."

Hassan Burani smiled. "Anything I can tell you . . . We are always told that we are ambassadors for our country."

"So you'll stay?"

"Oh, listen, Mr. Prescott . . ."

Martin Prescott said, "Martin."

"Martin? Yes?"

"Yes."

"Then I am simply Hassan."

"I'd no intention of calling you Mr. Burani."

They smiled at each other. Then Hassan continued. "You see, I have been in England before. And then I lived in houses, in rooms . . . Oh, unimaginable. Drab, damp, rotting; collapsing furniture, rents higher and higher because I was a foreigner and had to take what was offered me, week's notice here, neighbours complaining there—if I didn't take this I would have to have my head examined."

"Nice colloquial touch," Martin murmured.

"Oh, yes. That is one thing one learns in houses like that—colloquial English."

Martin grinned, nodded. "Fine. Fine. Well, I'm willing. You're willing. I've seen you. You've seen me and the place. Now there's only one possible hurdle."

"Hurdle?"

Martin stood up, clapped his hands together, rubbed dry palms against each other.

"You'll see," he cried. "You'll be confronted with the last hurdle, the last test, the final examination. Oh, yes. Now we'll go and have lunch."

They ate, chatted, arranged the rest of the day. It was therefore early in the evening that Hassan arrived back at the apartment, walking quietly up the stairs, breath easy, steps balanced, carrying two large suitcases to this second floor. Martin flung the door open, raised eyebrows, lifted one of the suitcases, whistled.

"A tough. A mighty man of muscle."

He ran Hassan into the hall, ho-ho-ing like some television pirate. At the far end of the hall stood a girl. With the point of her left shoulder she leaned against the wall. Her hair was long, chestnut, almost straight. Large, clear eyes, grey-green like a northern sea, watched the stranger, the round-faced, dark Hassan. She wore a woollen shirt, broad-striped in red and orange, then white trousers, tight about the hips. Her feet were bare.

Martin said, "Ricky. Miss Erica Mead. My fiancée."

"A fiancée is a mythical beast," Ricky said. She stood straighter, held out her hand. Hassan, advancing, took this and slightly bowed as he shook it, the movement stiff and strangely Teutonic.

"The hurdle," Martin cried. "You'd better make a hit with her. If she doesn't like you . . ."

"I spend a fair amount of time here. Martin hates raised voices." The girl said this almost belligerently, but with a small smile about the words as if to wrap them acceptably.

Hassan said, "Then we must quarrel in whispers," and the three of them laughed.

"Let's sit," Martin called out from the corridor. "We have a room for it. Come on."

Later, sitting, Ricky asked, "You're Muslim?"

"Oh, yes," Hassan said. "Though not fanatically."

"You're not going to start chanting in the middle of the night?"

"It only sounds like it. Actually, it is snoring."

"He doesn't look like a chanter to me," Martin put in.

Hassan shrugged. "Perhaps if you taught me I might turn out to be quite good at it."

Ricky laughed, leaning back into the black couch, amused at herself as much as at Hassan. But she felt herself to be in some subtle sense a pioneer, at the edges of her culture, her society, where its frontiers met those of an alien and perhaps inimical way of life.

"And food?" she asked.

"I take some from time to time."

"But I mean, sauces, powders, strange taboos . . ."

Martin laughed. "And cauldrons, incantations, powerful spells . . ."

Hassan shook his head. "It is powerful smells, I imagine, that are to be feared."

Martin laughed again, leaned across from his chair, slapped

10

in a congratulatory fashion Hassan's shoulder.

Ricky watched this contact almost as if uneasy. "Well," she asked, "will there be any?"

"Smells?"

"Yes."

"Nothing exotic."

"Powerful?"

"My Irish stew can sometimes be a bit strong."

Ricky nodded solemnly for a moment, then turned her head away, giggled. She looked down like some mildly guilty child. "I'm sorry," she said, "it's not just curiosity; later we'll know you too well and it'll be too late to say anything even mildly unpleasant."

Hassan laughed again. "That may depend on how well you know me."

All three leaned back, smiling. They felt something had been achieved, a contact had been made; a hurdle surmounted. Martin jumped up, strode vigorously to a cupboard, clattered glass.

"We ought to drink," he shouted. "Cement the union or whatever alcohol does."

"Ah," Hassan muttered. "Strange taboos."

"Of course," Ricky cried. "Islam, alcohol's forbidden."

Hassan smiled. "It's not really that—a lot of people don't really bother about it. It's a question of conviction . . . health —personal, anyway."

"Tomato juice?" Martin asked; he seemed for the first time a little cast down.

"Wonderful," Hassan said.

"That's a matter of opinion."

But he carried glasses, handed them with his usual flourish, then toasted, drank, ice ringing as it swirled to and fro in his whiskey. Hassan pursed his narrow lips, took small, blood-red sips, looked from Martin to Ricky, from Ricky to Martin, his dark eyes shining as if polished.

"Well, look here," he said after a while. "Those smells—I could cook tonight. Then you'd know."

"Tonight?" Martin looked at Ricky.

Ricky said, "We were going to take you out to dinner."

Hassan shook his head. "No. I'll invite you to stay in for dinner."

He jumped to his feet, glanced at his watch, nodded once, smiled round at them, then hurried out of the door. In a moment, they heard the front door shut, muffling the subsiding clatter of his busy feet as he ran down the stairs.

Martin moved from his chair, flung himself straight-legged into the couch. With a practised movement, his right arm curled about Ricky's shoulders; his left hand held his steady whiskey glass.

"Well?" he asked.

"He seems amiable."

"Even witty."

"Even that, yes."

"Of course, if you'd moved in . . ."

She shrugged. "We've been through that. There are formalities."

"A piece of paper."

"Not any piece—a marriage licence. Me lines."

"But three nights in five you . . ."

"That's different. That's sex; I need it and I love you. It would be ridiculous not to make the logical connection. But that isn't marriage."

"Nor is putting one's name to a ridiculous strip of paper."

"Oh, Martin, we've argued this one till it's become tramped down like some old playground."

"Yes," he said. "And as a result I was forced to get Charlie to share the flat. And then he was carted overseas by that petrol company. And then those queers came looking, three in a row. And then that embryo stock-broker . . ."

"Publisher," she said.

"Same thing. And finally Hassan, who's the first reasonable being who's answered the ad. All that because you refuse to . . ."

"Look," she cried. "I love you. That makes me more vulnerable than I'd like. But I can stand that; I believe, after all, that you love me. But I'm not going to give everything and find that you've given nothing."

"Nothing?"

"Martin, I love you. Do you think I don't know you?"

"Feckless, you feel? Weak? Not to be relied on?"

"Day-to-day. Happy in happiness. Unused to considering a future."

"I slave for that—for the future. Why do you think I spend night after night stabbing at endless bits of paper with endless bits of pencil?"

"Fame, recognition, vanity reinforced, money, self-awareness. And because, even if you get none of those in the end, in the meantime it lets you live without discipline, it allows you an image of yourself that doesn't damage your self-respect."

"What image?"

"That of a man with visions."

Martin closed his eyes, sighed heavily. He pouted at his whiskey, but did not drink. He felt a little bewildered by her honesty, almost as if betrayed. He did not really examine what she had told him.

After a while he murmured, "I wonder what sort of a cook Hassan is."

"Yes. I wonder too." She moved closer to Martin, leaned into him, sensed warmth and muscle. Once again he had escaped her, stepped away through his private fog into the endless muddled chambers of his haphazard character.

Hassan, in embroidered skull-cap and sweeping caftan, bearing brimming bowls of rice, of chunks of lamb in wild, red sauce, of cucumber salad and pimentoes, turned out to be a very good cook indeed. They ate in barbarian happiness, perhaps paining the fastidiously delicate Hassan as they scooped great mouthfuls of food onto crumbling lumps of bread torn off a French loaf, munching hugely between cries of friendly and enthusiastic appreciation. More quietly, they ate fruit, they drank the sweet, dense coffee Hassan made for them, they talked of how well the three of them got on together, of the evenings they would have, of the absurdity which was the myth of national differences and which they, by their happiness and their easy discussion were, they suggested, in the process of disproving.

"We should smoke a *nargile* now," Hassan said.

"Which is?" Ricky asked.

"The pipe, the water pipe."

"Hubbly-bubbly," Martin murmured.

"Even women?"

"Oh, yes," Hassan said. "Why not? Even women, sometimes."

"Emancipation?"

Hassan smiled. "It's a word. But with the veil, women were mysterious."

"And now?"

"Oh, now they must compete."

Martin laughed. "Especially the plain ones."

"Yes. More and more, the countries of the world grow like each other."

Ricky stretched. Under her trousers, her long thighs flexed, rounded, then relaxed. Her breasts lifted as her arms spread.

"Well?" she asked.

"Oh, you're *hors concours*," Hassan muttered. He and the girl smiled at each other.

"I'll go and wash up for that," she said, leaning forward.

"No. My evening," Hassan insisted, already on his feet, setting cups on a black tray, smiling, then turning, robe swirling, for the door.

For a short while Martin and Ricky listened to the distant clatter of crockery, the splutter of taps. Martin turned, kissed slowly Ricky's ear, licked its whorls and crevices, felt the small trembling of her body.

"Will you stay tonight?" he asked.

"What would your new lodger think?"

"He's not a lodger. And he's going to have to learn the facts of life some time."

"The facts of my life?"

"Our life."

"Ah. That life."

She leaned away from him, stood up.

"I was here last night," she said.

"You regret it?"

"No. But I've no intention of becoming one of your habits."

"It's worse than that. You're one of my needs, my necessities."

"Necessity's the daughter of frustration. You need me because I'm sometimes elsewhere. I think that's a fine state for the relationship to be in."

"It could be different."

"Happier. And stable."

Martin turned away, for the moment petulant. Then he smiled. "All that's nonsense, and you know it. If we lived together . . ."

"But you already have someone living with you. Or are you

about to rearrange Hassan's new life?"

Martin said primly, "I expect the conditions of my cohabitation with Mr. Burani to be in some essentials different from any possible cohabitation with you."

"Good," Ricky said, and walked to the door.

"You know that this whole subject is getting to be something of a bore?" Martin asked, in a low voice.

Turning, Ricky looked at him, her mouth suddenly a little pinched, a little bitter. "And do you know that we only discuss it on the nights when I won't stay?"

"But, good God, it's all . . . it's all market-place talk; barter. As if you were something, some object, a pretty tourist toy . . ."

"Yes," she said. "I know. There are men I'd live with and never mention licences—steadier men than you, or fly-by-mornings I'd only taken for the fun. But your vice is comfort; so I try and make you uncomfortable from time to time."

"But it's all so . . . I mean, there are how many tens of thousands of divorces every year?"

Ricky shrugged. "To divorce you've got to be full of money or of hatred—usually both. But people live together; then, suddenly they don't any more. One or other's moved away, drifted on, sailed off on a little wind of boredom . . . Well, I want to spend years and years and years with you—though at the moment I'm damned if I know why—and because comfort's your vice, marriage is the way to make sure that I will."

Martin stood up, ran a wide splay-fingered hand through his hair. "But marriage, marriage . . . I mean, the whole weight of this ridiculous society's in the word: all the bloody taboos, all the meaningless demands, the whole absurdity of a structure of relationships that's been cut off from any roots of instinct. It won't do. I won't underwrite it, I won't accept its institutions, its conventions, its endless damned pressures."

"It's me you'd marry, not society."

"In any case, to talk about permanence in a world like ours . . ."

"Oh, to hell with you," she said, laughing suddenly. "You and your clichés of rebellion . . ."

But seeing his face suddenly put out its lights, seeing the sudden sullen lines, she stopped. Martin sat down again, shrugged. Turning away from her, he stooped to light a cigarette.

15

He said, "You'll mutter some sort of goodnight to Hassan as you go?"

"Oh, I'm quite well brought up." She stood in the doorway, half-waiting, half only watching, but Martin said no more, did not look up at her.

"You'll work tonight?" she asked, not wanting to leave under his irritation's pressure.

"Oh, yes. Like every night—foregoing comfort, despite everything you think."

"I mean emotional comfort," she said, then snapped her lips shut, wishing she had refused herself the luxury of a last word.

"Yes, well . . ." Martin said, with a sort of furious vagueness.

"Goodnight, Martin, my love," she said, the words almost sighed rather than spoken.

"Goodnight."

She waited a moment longer, then turned, walked from the room. He could hear the sharp farewell she called out to Hassan and his darker mumblings of polite reply. Then the front door shut, decisively. He shrugged, settled more deeply into the couch. With his mouth drawn down, he had just begun a well-worn catalogue of misery and accusation when Hassan stepped cheerfully through the door.

Hassan said, "I would like to sit, talk a little, but really I am so tired . . ."

Martin abruptly stood up. "Yes, you sleep. I've got work to do, in any case."

"Work?"

"A civic centre."

"Of course. You are an architect."

"For a competition."

"You do much of this? Of this sort of work?"

"Petrol stations," Martin said, savagely.

"I beg your pardon?"

"I renovate them. I work in the architectural department of an oil company. Fifth desk on the left in the second row. I do designs for the renovation of petrol stations. To order, and to firm suggestion. That is, nothing of my own goes in at all. It's got to be anonymous or some petrol-hungry motorist might be put off by his miserable prejudices."

"So you work here to balance that?"

"I do small things. I did a little cottage up for a friend. *House and Garden* might do a feature—that would help."

"Yes. And so you enter these competitions?"

"This is almost the first. A civic centre for Sablecombe. That's on the South Coast . . ."

"Seaside resort. I know it. I was there once."

"Yes. Well, they want to go all civic pride and mid-century and so on, so . . ."

Hassan nodded. "Well, good luck," he said.

"Thanks. And you?"

"I?"

"You study. What was it—anthropology?"

"I'm doing a thesis on the unchanging elements of life in the Middle East. The bits of existence that have never altered. Why some have survival value and others not, or whether survival is just a matter of poverty and lack of opportunity for change . . ." He broke off, smiled again, shrugged. "I must be stopped when I begin to talk about it."

"Sounds interesting," Martin said, encouragingly; then he yawned. Both men laughed, Hassan reassuringly, Martin apologetically.

"But the meal was all right?" Hassan asked.

"Marvellous," Martin said, fervently.

They went out in the corridor, threw goodnights back and forth, then separated. The door of Martin's work-room shut; Hassan could hear the sharp click of a light being switched on. He imagined set-squares and drawing boards and the broad cleanliness of paper. He had a vision of Martin Prescott safely in his bubble of light and concentration. He smiled, walked softly to his bedroom.

.   .   .

Hassan Burani lay on the wide bed. The lime-green curtains were drawn. Beside the bed, a soft light glowed. Hassan was on his back. Slowly, methodically, he smoked, dropping the ash of his cigarette into an oblong stone ashtray which was balanced on his chest. In the near darkness, his dark eyes stared towards the ceiling. His time and the night were a screen. On it he watched a woman, fat, no longer young. Men in olive green stood on either side of her. Each held an arm. Beside them stood a third man. He carried a Skoda submachine gun. The woman looked over her left shoulder. She looked towards Hassan. Her mouth moved; she was calling out.

Hassan saw a neat figure, a man, a little plump, moustached: himself. He saw another, crouched, then running, arms reaching. He saw himself bend, sway sideways, avoiding those arms, tensing his own muscles. He watched the vicious lift and fall of his stretched hand and the other sprawling, then stretched across dust. He saw himself—neat, plump—turn again, the quick hand inside the jacket, then out. In his easy fist the snub barrel of a Smith and Wesson Special. Silently, it lifted and fell, lifted and fell; a thin smoke muddied the sunshine. Three momentary targets rose from behind a bank, then fell. In the heart-shaped centre of each, a hole.

A woman walked, trimly coated, through London rain. She came closer; lifting her beautiful face, beautiful chin and mouth, she asked for kisses. Hassan, alone on his bed, grimaced as dream Hassan bent in memory and offered the solace of lips and love and promises.

He turned, stubbed out the cigarette. Heavy tears stood in his eyes. He rubbed his face in his pillow, then lay still.

Outside, Martin, bleary-eyed from bending over Sablecombe Civic Centre, tip-toed down the silent corridor, glanced once, smiling, at Hassan's door, then stepped quietly into his own bedroom.

．　　　．　　　．

Hassan, yawning, set cups on the dark-red top of the kitchen table.

Martin, yawning, stood dressing-gowned in the doorway.

"Breakfast?" he asked.

"Two coffees are as easy as one. Of course, if you take tea . . ."

"No. Coffee, coffee; nothing less would do it."

Almost dazedly Martin peered about the kitchen. He felt suddenly warmed, as if he had been unexpectedly caressed. Someone cared for him. Someone was occupied with his needs, his preferences.

"You mustn't let this get a habit," he said.

"Breakfast?" Hassan laughed. "But I am deeply trapped by the habit of breakfast . . ."

"No. Getting it, putting it together. I mean, dinner at night, breakfast in the morning . . ."

"I have to make a good impression. It is the duty of a newcomer."

"I'm as new to you as you are to me," Martin said, almost irritably.

Hassan asked, "Is there any jam, any marmalade?"

"Blue cupboard," Martin said.

And, later, eyebrows appreciatively high, "Marvellous coffee," he murmured. He chewed, nodding delight; sipping coffee, he smiled as if coy across the cup's rim at Hassan opposite.

"What'll you do today?" he asked.

"Read, perhaps, like a good student," Hassan said.

"Here?"

"Or the B.M."

"The Museum! Of course. But then I can pay you for the coffee."

"Pay?"

"Certainly. By wafting you there in Nellie."

"Another lady? But, no, you say 'in' . . . Then it has to be a car. The machine personalised—an English virtue."

"An ancient monument, Nellie. A tribute to the past, a silent chastisement of the present, an assurance to the future that nothing is forgotten."

"It bangs a great deal and makes a lot of blue smoke?"

"It glides and if it has an exhaust I wouldn't be so indelicate as to look at it."

"Then it is large and entirely panelled in precious woods."

"Rare metals, leather from the skins of unimaginable beasts, fabrics woven by fairies."

"I accept your offer of a lift without hesitation."

In the deep and sober comfort of the Lagonda's back seat, Hassan looked down upon the pavements and tinny traffic of London. Motorists peered back at him, with the reluctant respect egalitarianism pays to wealth.

A taxi-driver called out, "Who are you then? Another of them Gulbenkians?"

Hassan smiled mysteriously, put one dark finger to his lips, shut his eyes. Then he picked up the brass-handled microphone which sat in a bracket below the left-hand window.

"I think we ought to get you a uniform, Martin," he said, "if we're going to this often."

"Delighted to wear anything you buy for me, sir," Martin replied, heaving at the wheel as if it were a ship's and waiting with some trepidation for the car's great length to respond.

Outside the museum a young man with long yellow hair turned to the girl beside him, and said, "There you are, love—that's how the Egyptians transported their mummies." Hassan climbed down, laughing, standing for a moment on the car's wide step to thank Martin, then watching and waving as the enormous Lagonda floated like a liner in the direction of Russell Square.

Inside the museum, the enormity of time oppressed him, the sterile industry of these busy northerners who had gathered so many fragments into this final meaningless, neatly-classified heap. The Assyrian Transept, the Egyptian Gallery, the Mausoleum Room, the Elgin Marbles—all separate from life and from each other, ripped out of all contexts, set aside from time, not allowed even to weather, even to moulder slowly under the weight of their millennia, to slide decently at last out of the awareness of men. African masks that would never again evoke gods or hide magicians; ploughs that had broken soil for Bronze Age man but now lay ridiculously below glass; Eskimo kayaks, far from fish; tomb furniture, stolen from a thousand thirsty ghosts now condemned to poverty and the ridicule of Hades; stone-eyed busts frowning their pride at strangers.

Hassan wandered below lion-headed gods; these tons of divine stone frightened him and, after a while, moving a little quicker, he passed out of their gallery. From the shadow of an enormous relief depicting a victory crucial to the happiness and progress of some dynasty long dust, a man stepped into the long morning light that lay across the stone floor. He was thin, dark, high cheek-boned, with a tall, narrow forehead above which grey hair neatly covered a long skull. He wore a dark-blue suit. He stared after Hassan Burani, his eyes too wide, too bright, too intent for comfort. Then, slowly, he walked in the direction Hassan had taken, standing for a moment beside a doorway, peering down the perspective of statues at Hassan sauntering in the distance, before stepping quietly through and to one side, putting between

20

himself and Hassan a multiple barricade of glass cases.

Yet, on the first floor, half an hour later, it was glass that betrayed him. Hassan had been bending, peering at the complex sexual gymnastics of Shiva and a shepherdess demonstrated in a series of bronze statuettes; straightening, he saw reflected the silver hair, the still, thin figure, even the glint of those insistent eyes. Giving no sign, he sauntered on, past a jungle of spears, pot-bellied wooden statues, Easter Island heads, staring masks, to turn at last into the Middle East again.

Babylon was about him, the signs of learning and of superstition, the marks of dynasties and priests. He walked on, more quickly now. Behind him he heard the shuffling of hurried footsteps. Then voices laughed about him, the clatter of insults; some class let out of school to investigate for an adventurous morning the relics of antiquity. Three blue-blazered boys ran by him and, suddenly, he was running too, careering past faded mummy-cases, rows of the serene, forever-bandaged dead, small models of the lives they had lived. His footsteps echoed among the echoes of those of running boys; one of these turned, looked at him in bewildered irritation. Hassan swung abruptly to his left, slowed, walked with long strides through Egypt and pre-history.

At the top of the north-east staircase he turned, glanced behind him. Two old ladies tottered towards him, one slow step at a time, smiling at each other in gratification, perhaps, at surviving alive the weight of all these thousand dead. Hassan took a deep breath, ran, long-striding, down the stair, taking the sharp turn with one arm flung out for balance. He hurried without stopping by petrified cascades of books, coming at last to the high drabness of the entrance hall and the monstrous pillars that guarded this cluttered past, to run again across the forecourt and the London spring.

At the main gate, he halted, looked left and right; then behind him. Grey hair shone in thin sunlight, thin brown face was turned towards him, neat black shoes moved in a quick one-two. A hand rose, as if in greeting; perhaps there was a smile between those strained and narrow cheeks. Hassan, swinging round, flapped his right hand at a taxi. Climbing in, he saw the man he had been fleeing begin to run. Perhaps his mouth opened, perhaps he called something . . .

21

"Quickly," Hassan yelled at the driver. "Quickly!"

The taxi pulled away, accelerated, swung left.

"Where to, then?" the driver called, leaning back to hear what Hassan ordered.

"Drive, that's all," Hassan said. "Here's a pound; drive till you've used up some of that."

"But I don't . . ."

Hassan opened the near-side door, stepped out of the driver's life; the man saw him run two long strides, stumble, then swing away. He shrugged. He'd drive for a few shillings' worth, seemed only fair; then he'd pick up the rest. That should warm his pockets; make his morning, it would. And there'd be something to tell the lads at the caff, after . . . He settled over the wheel.

Hassan, kneeling as if over a recalcitrant shoe-lace, peered through the windows of parked cars, watched his taxi disappear, watched the next one, a gleam of grey hair in it, a dark cheek, a thin body bending forward; smiling, he stood up, walked thoughtfully back towards Great Russell Street.

.　　　.　　　.

Down the corridor, Hassan's door softly shut. Martin stretched, walked to the sitting room window, watched for a moment the empty street below, defined like a river by its twin banks of lamps. Then he drew the heavy, oatmeal-coloured curtains.

"I like him," he said. "I really like him."

"He's nice," Ricky murmured, leaning gently sideways on the big couch, resting her cheek on her outstretched arm. "All those stories . . ."

"Entertainment as well as the shared rent. Arabia in the salon. The whole sockful—bemused Americans, palsied pilgrims wrong-footed for Mecca, double-bribed politicians, Sufi saints . . . Hollywood turns out to be the truth."

"He's nice," Ricky murmured again.

Martin nodded, slumped into a chair. "All the same . . ." he said.

"Oh, Lord. One of your moments of doubt."

"A thought, a fact. No more than that."

22

"Not attempted persuasion? I'm very tired—too tired to face arguments."

"No arguments. A fact: if I were doing better, there'd be no need to have anyone . . ."

Ricky interrupted. "Self-doubt? Self-persuasion?"

"Oh, just the life, the times. I asked Harrison if I could submit some ideas for the new branch headquarters in Glasgow."

"What did he say?"

"Oh, he smiled. It's a good smile, he must have worked on it, tried it in front of mirrors—one mirror after another as one by one they broke. It's a sort of metal smile, like Himmler's—as if he were copying a grimace he'd noticed was socially useful."

"What did he say?" Ricky asked again, curbing Martin's fanciful, dry-voiced bitterness.

"He said, 'I know what opinion you hold of yourself, Mr. Prescott. Fortunately the work that is assigned to you depends on the opinion I hold of you.'"

"You should leave there."

"Difficult situation—you know it is. I'd have to go for jobs in competition with the children who've just qualified. They can do most of what's wanted, and for less money. No, I've got to do something, have work to show, stuff completed . . . God, if I had a real career I wouldn't have to share my roof with anyone."

"Not even me?"

Martin turned towards her, looked at her as if he had never seen her before, never seen anything of such shape or weight or scent in his life. With her own eyes half-closed, she watched this examination; then slowly smiled. He leaned over her, hovered, held back, almost commanding, almost begging. Then with his right hand he lightly caressed her left shoulder, the soft skin of her neck, her ear-lobes. Almost indiscernibly, she shuddered; her lips parted slightly. Martin let his arm drop until it lay across her breasts, watched as her eyes dimmed and closed. He ran his wrist across her body in a caress so slow as to be almost perverse. Bending nearer he touched her dry lips with his own, then again. His hand took the warm bulb of her breast. Her deepening breathing rang in his ears like a tolling of bells.

"Oh, but Martin . . ." she murmured. "After all . . ."

But his hand stroked, kneaded; her lips pouted, a small frown

23

bit into her forehead as she concentrated on sensation. He ran his hand down the easy slopes of her belly; heat like a running tide followed his fingers, spread from their searching tips the length of her body. Muscles lost their function; she seemed all liquid, flowing where his caresses led.

His hand now curved over her knee, feeling the warmth of this, its firm roundness, the fingers slowly searching the soft skin just above. She lay deeper in the couch now, her head lowered as if for meditation; her face was almost hidden by the bright cascades of her hair. Slowly he stroked the long line of her thigh, the endless delicacy of its skin. She began to rock from side to side, her breathing short and deep, reduced to nothing more articulate than an occasional small moan. Convulsively she pressed her thighs together, then, turning her face into the cushions of the couch, let her knees fall wide, spread before him like some surrendered city.

Kneeling beside her, he kissed the long heat of her thigh. With his left hand, very slowly, he undid one after the other the six large buttons that held her dress together. Then she lay, her skin almost too white for him to bear against the deep black of the couch. Gasping, her head strained back, she could not restrain the demanding rhythm of her hips. Delicately he lifted the containing lace and nylon off her breasts; reaching, he kissed the down of her belly, the hollow between her breasts, then the pale, hard nipples.

"Oh, God," she sighed, almost sobbed. "Please, please . . ."

She raised her buttocks, her whole body a demand. Martin took the last of what covered her, the single strip of black that hid her, and with a single movement ripped it the white length of her legs. Kneeling closer, he stroked with his cheek the curled coarseness of her central hair.

"Please," she muttered again. "Please."

Suddenly standing, he slipped his arms beneath her, lifted her off the couch.

"What is it?" she whispered. "What are you doing?"

She tried for a moment to struggle, then slipped, to lie heavy-buttocked, helpless, in his supporting arms.

"What is it?" she asked again, almost plaintively, almost as if about to cry.

"This room is common ground," Martin murmured. "If

24

Hassan should . . ."

"Oh! Hassan," she said, wildly. "Hassan, yes."

Without another word, he carried her to the bedroom, put the light on, kicked the door shut behind him. In a moment the long throbbing moans of a woman love-transported came rhythmically through the door's yellow panels, to fade and fall like dying petals in the corridor's stillness.

      •   •   •

Ricky, pouch-cheeked about the breakfast toast, mumbled a question. Martin turned, holding in a flowered egg-cup a dark-brown, steaming egg.

"What's that?"

Ricky tried again. "What if you do well in that competition?"

"Nearly done, you know," Martin said.

"The egg?"

"The plans. Have to get a model made, though."

"Expensive?"

"Horribly."

"And if you win the thing; if you do well?"

Martin laughed. "Let's not be optimists. It hexes things."

Ricky shrugged. "It's too early in the morning for superstition. We haven't even looked at the papers. What if it goes well?"

"We could celebrate—have a holiday."

"If all the money's going to go on that model of yours, we might find the West Indies a bit out of the way."

"Well, there's a prize, of course," Martin said; then added, thoughtfully, "What about your old aunt's house?"

"Derbyshire!"

"I've never seen the Peak District. Cliffs, curlews, bracing breezes—why not?"

"I've not seen it since I was fifteen," Ricky said slowly. "It was wild then—no one's lived there for years. Or even had a holiday."

"But, if I remember, the old dame gave us a standing invitation."

"Yes. She did. And it would be a marvellous place to unwind."

"And wind again," Martin murmured. "And unwind for a bit and then, by golly, wind anew!"

25

"Is that indecent?"

"Probably, if it's fun. What about Derbyshire, then?"

"It's lonely—just an old house falling down, gorse, birds, great winds . . ."

"All Peter Scott and Outward Bound, then?"

"At least all that."

"Sounds marvellous."

She smiled. "Yes, it does. As long as we don't get to see too much of each other. There's no one and nothing there."

Martin smiled back at her, then sat up, egg loaded into a small, purple, plastic spoon. For a moment he watched this colour combination, then shrugged and said, "Why don't we take Hassan?"

Her face fell. "A threesome?"

"All right, let's amend the proposition. Why don't we take Hassan plus bird, if he can find one?"

"Provided we pass the bird as acceptable."

Martin grinned. "That sounds rather interesting—'Pass the bird, old chap . . . Ah, most acceptable.' Yes, provided the bird's a passable, clubbable beast."

Ricky nodded, the gesture firm, enthusiastic. "Done," she said. "A plan made."

Martin leaned over the table and kissed her with gruesome, egg-sticky lips.

Hassan, wide-eyed on his broad bed, heard them a little later scuttle, work-bound, out of the front door and down the stairs into silence. The flat seemed suddenly to contract, its stillness a threat or at least an emptiness, a sort of slate waiting for movement or perhaps even violence to set some mark on it. Hassan licked his lips, shifted to his left, to his right.

"I should get up," he murmured. "I should get to my feet."

Behind his empty eyes, the fat woman, her arms held by the strong arms of the uniformed, looked forever over her left shoulder, forever opened her mouth to call her silent greetings or appeals. The targets lifted, sat for a moment upright in his memory, were holed and blasted by the leaping gun in the right hand of memory's manikin, the crouched, remembered figure who had been himself. He saw this creature servile before a desk while a man with coarse hair and a large chin spoke to him, authoritative, threats in his smiles, his shrugs, his forcefulness.

26

He saw himself over and over again falling, being thrown, rolling, standing straight; to be struck once more, to fall and roll and straighten. He saw himself in his turn strike and leap and pull, saw others fall, some to stand again, others to writhe where he had dropped them. He felt once more the endless self-disgust, the pitiful sense of emasculating helplessness, the ferocity which only those moments had released, those quick impacts, the fleeting touch of body on body, the stress of muscle against muscle, the sudden solitude which meant success or victory.

With a sudden whiplash movement, Hassan was off the bed. He stood, lips compressed, in the centre of the long room. For a moment he hesitated, then walked to the high, natural-wood cupboard that stood against the opposite wall, rolled aside the door, took out a small, black case. He opened it, unlocking it with two separate keys, pulling apart its two halves—heat-resistant, harder than jemmies, to be no more than dented by explosions—to reveal the long pistol-barrel within, the strapped-down butt, the long, sheathed knife, the soft twists of plastic explosive, innocently held in place by cellophane, the three black notebooks packed with photographs of faces, of buildings, of apparently everyday street-corners bristling with the possibilities of ambush, the remaining pages filled with closely written notes under such headings as "Known Resorts", "Friends", "Skills", "Sexual Preferences". Hassan stared into the opened case, remembering the first weight of it in his hand, remembering threats, promises, plans, orders.

He walked slowly to the window. Spring still tugged at the hesitant leaves of the trees outside.

"I could take the stuff they gave me," he muttered. "I could just take it this morning, this moment; no problems then."

He thought of the small plastic container, flat, nestling now in a pocket of that opened case, thought of what it held, the three pills, the two small needles, each one the promise of a short pain and a long grave. He shrugged. He saw again yesterday's thin man, the grey hair, bright against the museum's pillars, the hurried approach, the meaningless smile on those thin features and the hand raised in imitation of friendliness . . . But the face changed, rounded; another person walked, smiling; warm arms spread, closed about his head, he swam in a secret sea of that remembered scent, her lips moved moist and insistent under his . . .

He swung away from the window, his face twisted by a sudden fury. Then he shrugged, licked his lips. Anger crumpled.

"But where should I go?" he asked himself. "What should I do?"

.   .   .

Ricky said, softly, "That rather renders the little woman superfluous."

She was standing in the kitchen's doorway, peering left and right into a new brightness. Someone had spent time on hard polishing, on sweeping and wiping and spiriting away dust and debris.

"You?" Martin asked. Ricky, turning, saw that he was speaking to Hassan, who had just came, shyly smiling, out of his room.

"Why not?" Hassan murmured. "I did not feel like work, so . . ."

"But it's marvellous," Martin cried. "Sensational. Miraculous housework, done by turning the back, like the fairy stories."

"Tales of djinn," Hassan agreed, laughing.

"And other strong spirits in bottles, to some of which I wouldn't be averse at the moment," Ricky said.

Hassan watched as she walked into the sitting room. Her breasts moved under a white blouse, her hips shifted inside the short black corduroy skirt she wore. Chestnut hair drifted as she turned her head, glanced once at him, then stepped towards comfort and whiskey.

"I think we should go out," she said, glass in hand, leaning against the heavy mantelpiece. She whirled ice in tinkling circles, then sipped. Under her brows, she glanced swiftly at Martin, at dark, round-faced Hassan. "I think we should go out this evening," she said again. "Martin. We haven't really gone out except to bolt one of those ghastly meals at The Droopy Cauldron."

"It's actually the Swinging Kettle, I believe," Martin said. He smiled at her, then at Hassan. "What about it, Hassan?"

"Me?"

There was a moment of silence in the room, a curious and for Martin almost inexplicable tension. Then Hassan shook his head. "Thank you, no, I have already bought for my dinner."

"But there's the damned icebox, for God's sake . . ."

"I don't think we should bully poor Hassan," Ricky murmured.

"Oh, it's not that—it's very kind . . ." Hassan smiled once at Martin, then for a long moment at Ricky. "Have a good time."

Then the door closed behind him.

Silence, then, in the sitting room. Martin and Ricky reflectively drinking.

"Is there, my love, something I've missed?" Martin asked.

"No, my love." Ricky finished her whiskey, set down the heavy glass.

"I thought there was a sort of heaviness, a sense of oppression . . ."

"How much of your life is Hassan going to share?" This was said abruptly, Ricky looking nervously at the far corner of the room.

For a moment Martin did not reply. Then he said merely "Ah!"

"He's here to share the flat. But if I want to go out with you . . ."

"The invitation was a little ambiguous," Martin said, carefully. "I misunderstood you. I'm sorry."

Ricky stared sullenly at the pale grey carpet for a moment. Then abruptly she smiled, stretched out, patted Martin on the shoulder.

"Let's go out," she said. "It's just my paranoia. Let's go out."

And they drove to town and saw Buster Keaton frenzied and frozen, chivalrous and foiled, in a grainy movie more modern than the National Film Theatre's careful decor, ate *lasagne verde* and drank a pale but mellow Orvieto in Soho, then returned, to find Hassan in robes playing once more his servile role.

"No," he cried. "I will make the coffee," rushing from kitchen to sitting room, bowing as he handed the dark-blue coffee cups, as he watched them sip, putting his hands together so that they almost disappeared in his wide, purple-embroidered, oatmeal-coloured sleeves.

Ricky said, "Hassan looks like a toy, standing there. One of those men you push and push, but who keep on rolling back, smiling . . ."

29

Martin said, "Sit down, Hassan. You ought to stay here. It's time we got you a coffee."

Hassan smiled, went out, came back with a small bottle of cognac.

"A present from the airline," he said.

"No. You bought it."

"Yes. But cheap."

Ricky put in, "Except that you don't drink."

"So, in a way, the price is cancelled," Hassan said, with a finality that almost disguised the lack of logic.

"Well, sit down, in any case; at least sit with us and . . ."

But Hassan was serving, bowing, almost kneeling. All the time he smiled; there was something hysterical about his movements, his smiling, as if he were under pressure of some kind, as if someone had under threat ordered him to behave as he was.

Ricky stood up. "Please," she said. "I can't stand that. You mustn't play the servant."

"On the contrary, I play the host," Hassan told her, softly.

Ricky shrugged, sat down again. "Then I'd like a cushion," she said, coldly.

For a second Hassan wavered, then his smile returned, he brought a cushion from a chair in the corner.

"And biscuits?" Ricky said.

Martin cried, "For God's sake, love!" But Hassan was already in the kitchen, rummaging in tins, returning with a plate of biscuits.

Ricky ate these in silence, looking in speculation at Hassan's now immobile face.

"A glass of water," she said, sharply, at last. Hassan looked for a moment surprised, then brought her one. Martin was sitting well back in his chair, his face to the ceiling, his eyes shut. Whatever game was being played by the other two, he had withdrawn from it, would take no part, not even as referee, not even as spectator.

Abruptly Ricky kicked off her left shoe. It dropped almost exactly in the centre of the room. She and Hassan almost slyly regarded it. They did not look at each other.

"Clean it!"

For a moment Hassan stood without moving. His mouth was set as though for fury. His right hand flexed, unflexed; perhaps he was on the point of stooping, of bowing and picking up the shoe, of taking it out of the room on the search for the necessary tins and cloths and brushes. But then he shrugged lightly, suddenly laughed. The sound was dry, like a motor not used for many months.

"Well, you are right. The *reductio ad absurdum*."

He looked up at Ricky, the two of them now helplessly grimacing in their laughter. They were like people who had been saved from a disaster. Martin slowly sat up, soberly looked from one to the other.

"Well, I must go to bed now," Hassan said. He smiled, nodded at both of them, softly went from the room.

He lay on his bed. He smoked his last, slow cigarette. From between the unrelenting uniforms, the fat woman appealed over her left shoulder, looked back, back down time at him splay-legged on the wide bed. The silver-haired man stood again outside the museum, his hand raised, signalling his ambiguous summons. Hassan turned his head, stared at the shadowed wall, remembering yesterday's panic, savouring today's expectation of fear.

The woman's face moved towards him, then abruptly swung away. He saw her naked on the blazing bedspread, her black hair spread like a peacock's tail about her head, her lips expectant, her fingertips touching as though to mark a direction the broad black flame between her thighs. Her face altered; Ricky's chestnut hair suddenly floated across a vacuum, her eyes smiled, one hand reached towards him in a gesture she had offered hitherto only from politeness but which might, one day, who knew . . .

Hassan stood up, stalked savagely to the window, flung it open, breathed as though he hated it the edged spring air; but breathed deeply, raising his face towards the bright metropolitan sky, feeling a forced calm spread over him like some containing film of plastic.

In the sitting room, Ricky said, "I have to go home tonight."

"Really? Home?" Martin murmured. He stroked her warm flank, the stretch of her thigh, the fall of belly, then of breast. "Really? You have to?"

"I want to," she said, suddenly standing up.

Martin sighed, let one lingering hand trail fingers down the long curve of her buttock. Then, lust dismissed, he too stood, thinking now of lines and measurements, of ventilation, light, sewage; thinking of his pencil's point decisive across paper.

"You still like Hassan, don't you?" he asked, though a little absently.

"Oh, yes," she answered. "Yes, of course I like Hassan."

PART TWO

Time flies, death urges, knells call,
heaven invites,
Hell threatens.
Edward Young

The evening sun flashed once through the bright early-summer leaves, hung for a moment tangled in chimneys, then sank under the weight of the world's darkness. Hassan stood silently at his open window. He held the fingers of his right hand tightly in those of his left. Slowly he turned from the dusk, began to walk softly, thoughtfully up and down the room. He thought of the town he was in, this tangle of London which held him like a web. He thought of the dangers of light, of identity, the chances of staying in shadow, faceless, while the years covered him with their fissures and barnacles. He sighed once or twice, shrugged, walked to the kitchen.

He was holding a just-washed glass to the light, correcting cloth in hand, when he heard Ricky's voice from behind him.

"In the kitchen again?"

"I enjoy housework. Like some people do exercise, I polish and . . ."

"Martin's working on his plans."

"Yes, I know. I heard him go in—what? Two or three hours ago."

"Yes. He works hard."

Ricky wandered nearer, trailing her hand on the blue plastic of the kitchen table. Hassan glanced at her, then nervously dipped plates in soapy water.

Ricky said, "How's your thesis going?"

"Oh, it progresses. It is slow work, of course."

"Of course."

"I mean, the problems are very complex. Agricultural methods, methods of storage, transport, the breeding of animals, systems of servitude, architecture, sewage disposal—oh, everything. One has to know almost everything."

"I'd like to read it."

"Of course. When it's ready . . ."

"Why not what you've done? You know, an outsider's eye can often help."

35

"It's very specialised. In any case, at the moment there are only notes."

"When do you write them down?"

"What?"

"I wondered when you worked best?"

"Oh, if there is something to be done . . ." Hassan murmured, clattering knives and forks, moving to and fro like someone busy.

"But you're always here."

"Ah, but when you are at work yourself, you see, I get down to it."

"But you never relax."

"Relax?"

"Go out."

"No. I do not go out much."

"You're always here. You're always dusting or cooking or . . . I wonder how Martin'd manage without you."

Hassan laughed briefly. "That is just a compliment," he said.

"Yes?"

"I do not do very much, really."

"Oh, enough. Enough."

"I hope so. After all, I am in the last resort a guest."

"The last resort?" Ricky stood suddenly still, looked at him very intently. "I wonder what you are in the last resort."

Hassan laughed again.

Down the corridor, a door slammed, Martin's voice sounded in a great cry. He came pounding towards the kitchen, giving the wall a series of enormous slaps as he did so.

"The last line," he shouted. "The last bloody opening door, the last west elevation, the last ladies' bog! It's done. It is written, it is laid down, it is ordered. Now all I have to do is get it there and then wait while they decide to give five thou. and barrels of kudos to some grumpy old knight who can't spend the one and doesn't need the other."

"It's finished?" Ricky asked. "Really? Done?"

"Real and done. Really done. Done real for real estate. Reels and reels of real estate, for reeling duns and dealing nuns and feeling Huns and doleful dons and . . . Well, no. For counting clerks and tabling taxes and mouthing mummers and . . . Come and see!"

36

The others followed him, to look as if knowledgeable through sheets of neat plans, idealised drawings, suggested details.

"And Nellie Two!" Martin cried, whisking careful cloths off his tall model.

"Now I see it," Hassan said.

Bending down to table level, Hassan peered, then nodded. At the back of the model, of the Civic Centre, rose the tall block, clear glass and black glass, of offices. To the right and in front of this, a long single-storey building sat behind tall windows and Portland stone.

"Marriages," Martin cried. "Dog licences. Health inspectors. The bureaucracy meets the public."

"And this?"

Hassan pointed to a white building dazzlingly cantilevered out above tiny multi-coloured cars. Its walls were windowless, broken only by ribs.

"Assembly hall," Martin explained. "Councillors in conclave. Glass-topped, air-conditioned—lovely. Higher than the other building, you see. So whichever way you look at it, there are levels, shifts of emphasis; under this, then out here . . . Or from here, you look through the hole—there's a park beyond, it'll be green, the councillors'll seem to be in a boat, you see, floating on the trees, on the treetops; that's right for a seaside town, after all. And I've used the whole site and still left space. You can walk under the council chamber to the park . . . Oh, it's lovely. They'll die when they see it, they'll kiss my feet, they'll wonder how it is that no one's ever heard my name!"

He sat down, abruptly covered his face in his hands. There was a moment of silence. Then he slowly shook his head.

"I shouldn't really tempt fortune like that." He paused again. "I'm thirty-four, you know. This business of time, of time passing . . ."

"It's a pity you had to sell Nellie, though," Ricky said after a longer pause.

"Oh, Nellie . . ."

"She paid for the model," Hassan said.

Martin suddenly sat up. "And the model will pay for a new Nellie. Nellie Three."

"When are you handing it in?" Ricky asked.

"Tomorrow."

She laughed suddenly, nodded. "Opportune, that—Paul Halling's giving a party. I meant to tell you."

"A celebration, then; a thorough launching!"

"Something like that."

"It was planned. The thing's an omen. Coming, Hassan?"

Ricky turned, suddenly paler. She stared at Hassan.

"No, I think I had better . . ." he began, then stopped. He looked for a moment at Ricky, his dark eyebrows high. He smiled. "But Ricky has been telling me I never go out. I have been chastised for this. Yes, thank you; yes, I would like to come."

Ricky swung abruptly away, bent low over the tall, gleaming model.

.   .   .

"I heard it from Hollander, and his cousin's in the P.M.'s office . . ."

"So I said to Paddy—well, he's gone all grand of course now that he's got the knighthood and everybody calls him Sir Patrick —but, anyway, I said to him . . ."

"The secret's to add the wine when it's already hot, and then a touch of marjoram and of course let it simmer absolutely for ever . . ."

"The take-over won't work, old man; tip straight from the boardroom—it just isn't on; you watch—tomorrow or the next day they'll simply collapse, right back to the sixty-two bob they started at."

"That's funny—I just thought you were looking a bit peaky; but now that you say it's a diet, of course . . ."

"Oh, God, but he's absolutely marvellous; stunning, overwhelming—I mean, he just takes something so totally banal and repeats it over and over again until you simply have to surrender; it's made the whole history of art redundant, that's what I feel . . . It vibrates, it leaps out at you—no one's ever done anything like it . . ."

"And then he put his hand on my thigh and I thought 'Oh Lord, here we go again' and I was just going to stand up and put on my captain-of-hockey voice when he simply swung me round and bit me in the . . . I mean, here, just here . . ."

DISCARDED

"I'm not snarling at you, but if you will sit in a corner with some chesty blonde I haven't even seen before . . . No, I'm not jealous, but you haven't come near me for two whole hours and that's not what I . . ."

Hassan, tomato juice in hand, walked between voices like a ghost through time. There were too many people about him, strangers shoulder to shoulder, obligatorily friendly, each optimistically presenting to the world some flattering censored version of a self they must have thought, given the lies they told, was fundamentally evil. He shrugged past heat and alien skin, came to a darker corner, stood for a moment with his back to conviviality; then turned.

The woman stood in the doorway. She faced him. Her grey-green eyes were wide as if with fear. She put her left hand to her hair, the long fingers trembling white against the disciplined and sweeping black. She was real.

Like a somnambulist—and indeed he had the sensation of one inhabiting his dreams—Hassan moved back across the room.

"Laura?" he said, leaning towards her, his voice soft, almost too soft for her to hear, "Laura?", long yards still between them, he approaching more and more slowly, as if he imagined that this time too her face and body would turn out to be no more than the habitual mirage.

"Osman!" the woman, Laura, said. Her voice was quick, breathless. "Osman—it's not possibly you. Not possibly; it can't be." She shook her head, shook, shook her head, the movement in some curious way giving a suggestion of hopelessness, of despair.

Ricky, passing, looked sharply at the woman, then frowned at the oblivious Hassan. For a moment, hesitating, she seemed about to speak, her right hand hovering as if to take Hassan by the sleeve. Then, suddenly biting her lip, she moved off among the guests.

Hassan said, "It's not right. Not fair. For months I stay away, I lock my door, shut up my life . . ."

"Months?" Laura looked up at him, her mouth turned down now as if she might cry. "Months?"

Hassan turned away, stood beside her, looked at the waves and ripples and thundering surf of the party as a man might stare sightless over oceans.

39

"I must explain, now. Now that we have met, I have to tell you why."

"No." Suddenly her voice was cold, her face rigid. She moved a little away from him. "No. It's too late for that, for any of that. For explanations."

"There was danger, you see. There were great pressures. I had to go away."

"Without a word?"

"Yes. Without a word."

She shrugged, pulled in her lips in an effort to control emotion, perhaps tears. "It's too late."

"Not to explain," Hassan muttered doggedly.

"I'm married, you know. Married, now."

There was a long silence. Then Hassan sighed, a deep, trembling exhalation. "Your husband is here?"

"No."

"You are pleased, happy with him?"

"Did you think I would spend the rest of my life nursing a broken heart?"

"I hoped you would not. But I could find no cure."

Once again there was silence, a long pause which they seemed to carry between them like a great weight. Then Laura abruptly opened her handbag, took out a small card.

"My address," she said. "I'll go soon. You stay, then come and see me."

"Tonight?"

She turned, still hard-faced, stared up at him. "Yes," she said. "Let's get it over. Let's have it finished with, once and for all."

She swung away and, like a graceful swimmer, lost herself among the party's buoyant waves.

.   .   .

Martin stood in the hall of the apartment; wrapped in darkness, he held Ricky in his arms and kissed her.

"You're drunk," he said when he had finally leant away to fumble for the light switch.

"Oh, yes," she said. "Oh, quite drunk."

She put out both her arms, stroked Martin's hips with long

tense fingers. He stood apart from her, his eyes half-closed like a cat's under these caresses. Then, violently, he stepped closer, put one arm about her, led her to the bedroom. They fell in a flurry of leg and skirt across the bed; her black-stockinged thighs splayed to his hand's prompting, his shirt ripped as he tore it from him, her dress and slip fell like soft parachutes to the grey carpet.

Their bodies white to white rolled towards the long pillows, his hands over her like some demented pianist's across a keyboard, she with toiling buttocks shouting her passion. Order reaffirmed itself, rhythm; then the last howl of joy; then silence.

After a long time, slowly, Martin climbed out of bed, took cigarettes from his jacket pocket, lit two. On his way back to the bed he closed the forgotten bedroom door.

"It's as well Hassan wasn't there," he said.

"I shouldn't have noticed," she muttered in a thick voice. "Wouldn't have seen."

"He would have."

"Wouldn't have looked. Anyway, his name isn't Hassan."

"Isn't?" Martin leaned on his elbows, looked through the darkness at the pale gleam that was her face and shoulder.

"Heard a woman speak to him tonight, someone he knew and I didn't."

"Someone he knew?"

"No need to be surprised. After all, he's been in London before. Might meet old pals anywhere."

"I suppose he might," Martin agreed, keeping something of surprise in his voice.

"This old pal called him Osman."

"Osman?"

"Osman. No doubt about it."

"Odd."

"Yes. Thought I'd mention it."

"I wonder where he is?"

"Ah. Where?"

She crushed her cigarette in a large ashtray of black glass, rolled towards him, put one thigh over his, began gently to nudge him with her belly.

Hassan, elsewhere, stepped cautiously from a taxi, looked almost furtively left and right as he paid, then watched the large red rear light of the disappearing cab swing away, past tree-shadow and patches of lamplight until, like a distant cigarette gone out, it whisked out of sight round a bend. Slowly he began to walk through silence. Houses, like dark, complacent packages of prosperity, stood back from the pavement, protected by privet and curved, rudimentary drives. Here and there a lit, mock-antique lantern illuminated the red paint and wrought-iron decorations of a front door. In the intermittent midnight breeze, trees rustled, drew monstrous shadows across the light of street lamps, softly clattered small branches together.

Hassan stopped outside an iron gate. For a long moment he stood there, his head down; he might have been in prayer. Then he took a deep breath, rammed the gate open, walked with foot-steps heavier and more assertive than usual up the flagged path. Briefly, he pushed the bell button. In a moment the front door had opened. Laura stood in light, her face tilted to look up at him, her expression sombre. For a moment they watched each other, almost like two antagonists searching for the signs of incipient defeat. Then she stood to one side, made a slight movement of her free hand. Hassan walked into the house, this well-appointed home, this careful stage-set for a marriage. Laura closed the door behind him.

In the house opposite, almost invisible in the darkness, a small movement: the easy flutter of an upstairs curtain falling into place. Then a light beyond the curtains, mildly picking out the red and purple leaves of their bucolic pattern. After a minute, the light went out; there came the click of a lock, a hinge softly in movement, a door shutting, briefly footsteps. Then silence.

"Well?" Laura asked.

She sat in a wide, pale-green armchair. In a negligent left hand she held a cigarette. Her grey-green eyes watched its blue smoke lie across the dead air of the room.

"Is this the man?"

"Yes."

"He looks . . . No. I don't know how he looks. He is a mystery, something I find difficult to understand."

"Best say nothing."

"Yes. Nothing."

"Best talk about yourself."

She looked away from him now, busied herself in tapping

ash into a pink porcelain rose. He turned from the photograph, the sideboard it stood on, walked restlessly to the dark-green velvet curtains, flicked at them nervously two or three times, then moved uncertainly towards the heavy, tasselled couch that stood in the centre of the room.

"Myself," he murmured. "Well, myself, of course . . ."

"Without a word," she said. "Without a word, then. Perhaps now you should say."

"Where to begin?"

"Where it began. Why did you leave?"

"They called me back."

"Who?"

"The government. I was a student, they were paying for the university."

"That doesn't . . ."

He interrupted. "They asked me to come back and I refused. They said they had need of me. I said I had need of education. They said they would cut off my grant. I said I would work, in that case; stay here and find work, unofficially if necessary."

"You told me you had troubles. You said at the time there were problems with your grant, your government."

"Yes, troubles, problems . . . They arrested my mother."

"Mother!"

"Yes."

"But why?"

"To coerce me."

"With no reason, no charge, no legal? . . ."

Hassan laughed. "To be British is to be very safe, to believe a great deal in the power of words like 'legal'. But they are all lies, those words, because the reality they pretend to is just a gift, something lent even, something which can be taken back again by the men of power from whom you have borrowed it. It is the men who make the laws who give a reality to words like 'legal', and when those men are not honest, are not concerned with legality . . ."

"Yes," she nodded, bent again over the ashtray. "I see."

"Perhaps."

"But when your mother was in prison, when they'd taken her, why didn't you come to me and? . . ."

"Because then I knew that it was special, that it was something more than a broken regulation. Then I got frightened you see; I began to worry. Because they wanted me back very much indeed. I thought that it was something very bad, but I had to go because of my mother. I walked through the streets—twice I walked to your house, walked to the gate and past it and then back again and in the end away, home—trying to make my mind up what to do. I thought that whatever it was would be secret and perhaps dangerous—maybe they would arrest me, shoot me for I cannot imagine what crimes. So in the end I went."

"Without a word."

"Yes. I just went. I did not want to tell you lies, I did not dare to tell you the truth. Because if there had been some sort of scandal, a word in the newspapers, perhaps, or even a letter from you to the embassy . . . I would still have had to go, because of my mother, you see; but after a fuss it would have been very much worse."

"You didn't trust me, then?"

"No. I did not trust you to keep quiet, you see, to make no effort to help or save or . . . I did not trust you not to interfere."

"Yes." This was said blankly, nervously. Hassan moved nearer, stood looking down at her.

He said, "I knew you, after all."

For the first time, faintly, she smiled. Looking up at him, she shrugged slightly. "And what did they want to have you back for?"

"To make a murderer out of me."

The silence surrounded them like a desert. She shut her eyes, unable to face her lack of understanding.

"A murderer?"

"There are exiles here, dangers to them. Consider it from their point of view. I spoke English, I knew England, London. I was acceptable to the authorities; that is, they had no reason to be suspicious of me, to be worried if I went away and then came back. I seemed an ideal assassin."

"But they didn't know you."

"They did not need to. They held my mother. And like everyone, I was in the army when I was seventeen. They looked up records, I suppose; I can shoot, after all, I had no difficulties with their courses, with the training. From their point of view, there was nothing wrong with me. I was healthy, I could be taught

44

what I did not know; with my mother under threat of death, I could be levered into willingness."

Another world, she thought. In the hall outside, gently a clock struck the half hour. Savagery, distance . . . He is very alien from me, she thought.

"So when you went back? . . ."

"I saw my mother. Then I did what I was told."

"The training?"

"Yes. The training."

Again he saw himself, hand raised, then chopping down. He saw the targets lift, shred, disappear. He saw the filled notebooks his case hid, the blank faces of the intended victims.

He said, "Then something happened that they had not foreseen. A man in a café, a note slipped to me. 'Your mother is dead.' "

"Dead? In prison; she died in prison?"

"Her last desire was that I should know. She understood why they had taken her. Dying, she released herself and me."

He saw the woman, fat, afraid, turning to her left, craning over her shoulder, silently mouthing words he had not been there to hear.

"I never saw her again, you see. After I came to London that first time. She had expected to be proud of me."

"You left them, then? You stopped training?"

"No. They would have killed me."

"Yes." She wondered at the ease with which she accepted the possibility of murder. "You'd either be useful to them or nothing. Worse than useless."

"Dangerous."

"Yes. I see that."

"So I finished it. All the hitting, the shooting, the suffering, the false interrogations, the techniques of death. Then they sent me back to London."

"Again, no word."

"Yes. No word. How could I put you in my danger?"

"Danger?"

"I was to have been met at Victoria Station—they thought as a student I should not fly. I was to have been met there and told my orders. It was all arranged—passwords, appearance, everything. But I did not stand at the corner of that bookstall, I did

45

not wait, I went another way and hid myself in London."

"Hid?"

"Among ten million people, even a Middle Eastern personage like me is not so very remarkable. I shared a flat with an architect. I was very nervous. I tried to take up my old life."

"No. Not all of it."

"I mean, my work. It was a mistake. I went to the British Museum. They were waiting for me."

"They? But they didn't know what you . . ."

"Oh, this one did. They must have sent for him at once. He knew me. He had helped train me."

The grey hair gleamed, the hand came up in mock-friendly salutation.

"What did they say?" she asked.

"Nothing. I managed to get away from them. Since then, I have stayed away from there, from anywhere I knew. I have stayed in the house. I have been bored, afraid; I have thought of suicide. I prepared a hiding-place, up in the north—my one trip out of London. Should I go there? I no longer know what to do. Tonight was the first time that I have gone out—my friends asked me to go with them, this architect and his fiancée. So I met you—good luck, bad luck . . ." He shrugged. "But we met."

Again the silence stretched about them, between them. Nervously, she lit another cigarette. She leaned back, crossed her legs. Almost absently, he looked at the slope of her knee and thigh; after a moment, she pulled her skirt down.

"It's very hard to believe."

"Yes," he said, simply.

But she knew it was true; he had been as excited and relieved and afraid as she when they had met, had been too honestly eager to see her and speak to her to tell her lies now. He need have done none of it, or spoken briefly of some woman elsewhere, of a marriage arranged, of family duty . . .

"Where is your husband?" Hassan asked. He sat at last, falling back as if unbearably tired into the deep cushions of the couch.

"Newcastle," she answered.

"Why?"

"He's a constructional engineer. They're building something

46

up there—a factory or a power station . . . I don't know."

"You are not concerned about what he does?"

"I married him because I'd been in love with you and suddenly where you'd been there was just this enormous hole. Nothing. And before that, there was Ken."

"Who died."

"You remember?"

"Yes. You told me."

"So I thought, this time it's got to last and it's got to give me a little peace and if he's solid and dependable and strong he'll do for me."

"He is all these things?"

"Yes, Solid, dependable, strong."

"Rich?"

"He isn't, but he makes a lot of money."

"Boring?"

"Yes. He's boring."

"So you're? . . ."

"Anaesthetised. Don't talk about happiness or love—or even sex, lust . . . All that's another dimension. I've stepped out of all that, out of that sort of expectation. My life's steady, regular —and so am I. I'm in my life, I've grown into it; I fit it very well now."

Hassan nodded, then slowly stood up.

"But now I am here. I am in your life."

"Yes," she said, noncommitally. "You."

He shuffled slowly towards her, his feet silent on the deep carpet. She watched him, her eyes wide and wary. When he was close to her, he bent, very softly kissed her on the left ear. She felt his lips warm against her skin, dry, firmly caressing. All that she was flowed towards his touch; it was as if he were summoning some new and wider self, a person she had thought no longer existed; a sort of ghost. His hand moved over the curve of her shoulder; she shivered, then looked away. She sat without moving. His fingers moved through her hair, their touch hesitant and tender.

"No," she said.

"No?"

"Really. I can't . . . Seeing you, suddenly coming across you . . . If it's revival, a rising from the dead, then I can't cope

47

with it. Really. I can't cope with it yet."

"But we will meet again?" His voice was low, his lips still near her.

"Yes. Now we have to. Haven't we? I mean, we must."

"Must. Yes."

"I'm often alone."

"Your husband? . . ."

"He's off; buildings and bridges and, oh, foundations and girders take him away. They're always taking him to some God-forsaken corner of Europe."

"So we will meet."

"Yes."

He moved closer, put his arms on the two arms of the chair. She felt as if enveloped in his warmth, in the warmth and the desire that came from him, that spoke to her across the long, empty months. She turned away, shook her head. Gently she pushed him aside, then stood up.

"You must go."

"I can telephone you?"

She gave him her number, led him to the door.

"I could call a taxi," she suggested.

"No. I will walk. Later, perhaps, I will see one."

For a moment they smiled at each other. He kissed her on the cheek, then left, walked quietly into the night. With his head down he walked through darkness, the shadow of trees, the regular dribbling of light from the high lamps above.

"She said 'Not yet'," he thought, with a kind of jubilation. He did not notice, wrapped in hope and dreams, the steady secretive footsteps that matched his own as he traversed the night.

.   .   .

"Hassan, Hassan—morning's flung a bloody stone into the bowl of night, Hassan. What's to be done about it?"

Out of tiny eyes, surrounded by the wrinkles of pain, Martin Prescott regarded his dazzling kitchen, the glitter that was daylight, the busy, unsteady Hassan.

He said, "You're about, Hassan; buzz, buzz, buzz, I wonder what it does—that's you, buzzing about, hither, then thither . . ."

"What it does," Hassan pointed out, "is coffee."

Martin nodded wearily. "That's the name of the stuff," he said and slowly sat at the kitchen table. Hassan put a mug before him and he drank black liquid; then more; then leaned back, sighing, rubbed his eyes wearily with his left hand.

"Dreary party," he murmured. "Dreary, dreary party."

"It seemed typical of the week-end recreation of a certain section of the British bourgeoisie."

Martin laughed, sighed again, then nodded. "Yes. Typical."

"Toast?"

"I'll make it." But Martin sat where he was, made no move.

"It's done," Hassan said. He dropped brown slices on a pale-blue plate, spread butter, set all before Martin.

"It's late, I suppose?" Martin asked, his teeth littered with crisp, then disappearing, crumbs.

"After ten."

"Christ! And Ricky's gone?"

Hassan smiled. "If you have not seen her, she's gone."

"Yes." Martin nodded, ate, drank. "She said you met someone you knew."

"Used to know. A woman."

"Ah! Woman!"

Meaninglessly, they smiled at each other, then both dipped towards food.

"Ricky said this woman used some other name."

"Yes. Osman," Hassan said, steadily.

"I see. Good name. Why?"

"Because it is my name."

"Nonsense. Your name's Hassan. You can't tell me—knew you since you were a baby tenant."

Hassan pursed his lips. "They are both my names. Hassan Ali Osman ben Abdul el Burani."

"A mouthful."

"Quite."

Martin nodded in a satisfied way for a moment, then said, "Why does she call you Osman? Or why did you present yourself here as Hassan?"

"She did not care very much for Hassan. I offered her all my names to widen her choice. She picked Osman."

49

"Why?"

"She thought it was less hackneyed than Hassan. She said people would never believe she had an Arab friend called Hassan, they would simply imagine she had seen too many films."

Hassan was speaking more quickly now, perhaps a little nervously. But Martin did not notice. He ate stolidly, wiped his mouth, pushed the plate to one side.

"What's her name?"

"Laura."

"You're quite happy to call her that?"

"Oh, yes. Quite happy."

Martin laughed abruptly, then stood up. A few minutes later he called brisk farewells, ran for the front door, the Underground, work. Hassan sat without moving for a long time. He thought of Laura—a Laura who smiled at him, then turned away; a Laura hard of face and voice, demanding explanations; a weeping Laura, sitting in some darkness, suffering the secret of his desertion; Laura naked, spread for love; but for whose love? He thought of Laura married. With a grimace of pain he stood, took the plates and cups from the table, carried them to the sink. His hand was on the hot tap, the fingers tensed to twist it, when the doorbell rang.

When Hassan opened the front door, the grey-haired man had already set his polite smile in place. He nodded, walked into the apartment.

"You are alone?"

Hassan slowly shut the door. He let his fingers lie along the cold metal of the lock, watched them for signs of fear. They lay steadily, as if he were relaxed.

"Yes. I am quite alone."

I am, he thought; am quite alone, am cold, unconcerned, beyond fear. He was surprised to discover no feeling in himself, no turmoil or flurry; he was empty, peaceful, waiting to be filled with purpose.

"In here?" the man asked. He stood at the sitting room door, nodded briskly.

"Yes. In there will do quite well."

Hassan sat in the couch. He felt its length stretch away to the left and right of him; for the first time he felt vulnerable, too exposed. He struggled against this sensation, realised for a moment how near fear was; then settled again into calm.

"You are well?"

The grey hair moved nearer, dark eyes looked as if in concern out of the thin, high-cheek-boned face.

"Very well."

"You are not working on the thesis?"

"I have been working on my notes. I have been ordering my ideas."

"Ah. Your ideas."

The man took out a ribbed silver cigarette case, took out a cigarette, put the case away, lit the cigarette with a lighter which matched the case. He made no gesture towards offering a smoke to Hassan.

He said, "Those ideas . . . What are your ideas?"

"About what, specifically?"

The man smiled. Lines cut his lean face into fragments and splinters; it looked as if it might fall apart.

"Yes, the specific—there speaks the student." He paused, looked about the room. "You are comfortable here?"

"Yes."

"It is different from what I might have chosen."

"I suppose it would be."

"It is not what I chose for you."

To this Hassan made no reply. His large eyes watched the other man intently. He listened with passionate attention to every soft syllable the other let drift into the room.

The man said, "You did not go to the place that was chosen for you."

"No."

"And the work you were sent to do—you have not done it."

"No."

"Are you near doing it?"

"No. Nowhere near. It will not be done."

"Oh, I think it will. Perhaps not by you—or perhaps by you after all."

"Never by me."

"Your mother, after all, depends on you. Entirely."

"She depends on God."

"Ah. God."

"Entirely."

"She is frightened, God's interest or not. She thinks you have betrayed her."

"She cannot be betrayed. She is dead."

"Dead!"

The thin man stared for a short moment at Hassan; his eyes hit like strokes of lightning, then moved elsewhere. There was a short pause.

"Who thinks she is dead?" the man asked at length.

"I have heard she died. I heard this months ago."

"Months ago"—this said slowly, thoughtfully—"yes, months ago. And so no rendezvous at the station, no tenancy of the prepared apartment—and the work left undone."

"There was no need. My mother was dead."

"She was not."

He said this very firmly, the words spaced out to give them emphasis.

"The men who told me had no motive for lying."

"I expect they did not have much enthusiasm for the government as at present constituted."

"They knew that such a lie would kill my mother."

"They knew that the truth would kill the traitors who are hiding here in Europe."

"No. They spoke to preserve me, to undo force."

"Nevertheless, they lied to you."

"I cannot believe that."

"Your mother lives."

"No. I do not feel that she lives. I think she is dead."

The man said, "We have looked for you for several months."

"I knew you would."

"We had hoped to persuade you."

"I cannot be persuaded."

"What if we took Laura? What if we held her as we hold your mother?"

Hassan said, still calmly, "You cannot take Laura because here you are in a foreign country and the difficulties are very great. You do not hold my mother because she is dead."

The man said, in his voice now the edged sounds of anger, "You are a member of a special and highly-trained unit of your country's army. I am your superior officer. You have been given a task and I order you to fulfil it."

"I cannot . . . will not obey that order."

The man stood up. "We cannot afford your cowardice," he shouted. "To save yourself you are prepared to kill your mother. But we have no time to give you, we cannot permit you the luxury of matricide. We need a return on the money and the months that have been spent on you."

"There will be no return."

"There must be. The safety and stability of a country is at stake; perhaps that of a whole area, the whole Middle East. Perhaps of the world." The man stood closer, leaned over Hassan. "It has to be done; the things you have been ordered to do must be done."

"I am not a murderer," Hassan cried. "I do not want to kill. My dreams are of blood, of my hands killing . . . I am not a murderer."

"Yes, you are," the man said, his words bitter. "That is what you have been made into. You are a murderer. Now I order you to fulfill your vocation."

"I have no vocation! There is no vocation! I did what you asked because of my mother. But my mother is dead."

"She is alive," the man shouted. "And she expects that you will save her. You thought you could hide—from us, from her, from what you have to do. But you have been found, you will be made to save your mother's life, her dignity, her sense of old age and of respect . . ."

Hassan stood, faced the thin-faced man. "I would like you to leave."

There was a silence. The thin man stepped slowly backwards, his eyes on Hassan.

He said, "You refuse an order?"

"I am glad to be able to," Hassan answered. "My life belongs to me. You thought you could buy it with my mother's, but that was an offer made in a weak currency; it belongs to a time which is now bankrupt and done with. Now there is a new time, a different moment; in this moment, you cannot coerce me. I will not do what you want."

"You refuse an order, then?"

"I want to be left in peace. I want to go back to study, to think of books and millennia and ancient methods of ploughing the soil. I have nothing to do with assassination, with killing; I want nothing to do with that."

"So, yes, you refuse an order?"

"Yes. I refuse it."

The thin man nodded a slow acceptance of this defiance. Then, swiftly, he was in movement, his hand like a striking snake lifting towards his shoulder and the concealed pistol. But Hassan, already waiting, flew. His body horizontal to the ground he slammed like a projectile into the other's chest. Both men fell; the gun thudded on carpet. Hassan rolled, stood again. The thin man, still a little breathless, made his single mistake. His head turned, he searched—as if he had time, as if there were distance—for the gun. Hassan moved again, he leaped forward, he kicked, then chopped down, he moved like some storm, like some incontestable force of nature. The thin man choked; blood stood in his nostrils, along the line of his lips. Hassan's bladed hands blurred, struck. The thin man fell away, tore once at the bland carpet; then died.

Hassan panted, the breath catching in his throat as if from pity.

"Come on," he said, "come on. Get up; you must leave."

The stretched arm did not move; the fingers were spread like claws across the carpet's pile. The grey hair shone brightly in the pale sunlight.

"Get up," Hassan said. "Get up." But his voice was uncertain. Once again he whispered, "Get up," but he knew the man would not get up. For a long time he stood staring at the body, still panting, his small mouth hanging stupidly open, saliva rolling down his round chin; he could feel his heart beating, yet could not believe that he was really present, that this situation existed in reality and that he inhabited it.

"But you must have known I would not," he muttered at last. "You must have known."

But he understood that the man, knowing this, had come to issue no orders or to insist on the fulfilment of no bargain: he had come to execute Hassan.

"What could I do?" Hassan asked. "If you had not come in, had not found me; if you had not . . ."

His voice trailed away; slowly he licked his lips. He turned from the body, began slowly to walk about the room, touching small objects as if to reassert normality. He did not look down,

54

did not consider the dead man; it was as if he hoped that the details of the ordinary would close over the moment like water, that when he finally turned round the body would have sunk through time as if through water, as if buried at sea.

But it was there, the right trouser leg rucked up a little, the soles of the shoes showing their patches. Hassan, turning, kicked metal: the dropped automatic. He looked at it for a long time, now and then shaking his head. It was to have been his noose, his guillotine, his firing squad. In its barrel, there lay a death for him. Abruptly he picked it up, put the muzzle to the side of his head. He could feel the cold of that metal circle strike through his hair. He sighed, put the gun in his pocket. Should he leave now, go north, put water and a closed door between himself and the nemesis of which this man had been the messenger? Or had he, by this killing, once and for all out-distanced his enemies? He stared at the carpet to the left of the body; he would wait, he would be watchful, he would leave when the moment was right. Through lightly-pursed lips, he began an almost silent, nervous whistling.

Finally, bending, he took the body by its arm-pits, dragged it through the door and down the passage into his own room. There, holding it in this way, he stood for long minutes, frowning as if thoughtfully, encased in silence, irresolute. He felt, he thought, a little feverish; he became suddenly aware of a great need to urinate. As if in sudden distaste, he threw the body to one side. With fastidious toe-tips, he pushed and rolled it under the bed.

In the sitting room, briskly, he tidied, rearranging furniture, checking for fallen objects, punching into shape disarranged cushions. When all was back in order he went to the kitchen, slowly washed up the dishes he had begun. This finished, he stood still again. He was, perhaps, a little dazed. Without moving, he stared at the floor.

Then, turning, he seemed to recapture resolution. He rushed from the kitchen; in a moment, the front door had slammed behind him and he was running down the stairs.

.   .   .

"It was so easy. That was the thing. Easy, easy—it was so simple."

55

"Why should I help you?"

"I could not help it. Once I had begun, once the movements were in my hands . . . It was as if I was captured by something —by other powers, some sort of will . . ."

"I can't think what I can do—I can't imagine why I should."

"It was easy. My hands simply moved, then he was dead. This, then that . . . He was dead. He was lying there. Now you have to help me."

"Why? Why should I help you?"

"It was what they taught me, you see. But it was so easy. A sort of power—it means something, it is very dangerous, very, very dangerous . . ."

"Why?"

This word, shouted, stopped him. He stared as if disconcerted not to find himself alone. Facing him, Laura stood, pale, her lips moving as if she might begin to weep, her back very straight and rigid.

"It is very dangerous. I can feel it; it is very dangerous for me. I do not want to be alone with that."

"But it's murder! Haven't you realised that?"

"No, I mean help . . . help me . . . Not as you think. I need no help with the murder. I want something to act against the feeling, I want to . . . to unlearn the power; there is knowledge here I would rather not have. Can you understand me?"

"I can't think what you want of me. You talk about help— are you trying to say that you didn't kill him? That the story was nonsense?"

"No."

"But you come here, you burst in here . . . I mean, you tell me about the man, about this man, you say he's dead, you want help . . . I don't know what you want!"

This last was said loudly, forcefully; there was an edge of hysteria in her voice now. Hassan looked at her out of wide, empty eyes; their blackness was like that of space, infinite, beyond possibility of limits.

"You do not understand what I mean?"

"If you want help . . . I mean, I can understand that you . . ."

"Yes. Help."

He nodded decisively, turned away from her, walked to the

window. He looked out into the garden, not seeing the easy movements of the flowers against the summer breeze.

"All right," he muttered. "If that is all there is."

"All?"

"That I may not be understood—yes, all right: I am understood. How about that?"

She shook her head, shrugged in despair. "I don't know what you want."

"Help," he said, turning towards her, his movements abrupt and nervous now. "Your help to save me. I must hide the body of this man. I know no one who can help me but you."

"And I—why should I?"

"Because you have made another life and will be happy, you have made a new future for yourself, while I have no life now and no future. And more directly, perhaps, because they only found me after I visited you."

"They were here? They were watching?"

"I have no faith in coincidence."

"Watching me? Waiting for you?"

"It was one method, after all. You do not think it makes sense?"

"Yes." She nodded, looking down as if in some obscure manner guilty herself of a betrayal. "Yes. It makes sense."

"So you will help me?"

"I must."

"How?"

She took a deep breath, licked dry lips, then took a short step nearer to him. Her face was pale still, but its expression now very firm and determined.

"I know a place. But you must get . . . it . . . you must get it to me. I'll take the car, I'll wait for you. But I'm not coming up. I won't be seen with you."

"I do not want you to be in trouble."

"No. I don't want trouble. I asked you here and so they found you and I suppose in a way that involves me, but . . ."

"Where shall we meet?"

"Somewhere near you, I suppose."

It was forty minutes later that, sitting nervously behind the wheel of her red-and-cream Triumph, she saw him, half-bent by the weight, coming down the pavement with on his shoulder a dark-brown trunk.

"In the back seat," she said, her voice low, tense, as he hesitated beside the car.

He reached down, opened the door, let the trunk slide heavily until one end lay on the seat.

"Quickly!" she snapped; her voice was dry, almost at the limit of control. She saw her hands—whose hands, she wondered, staring at them—trembling as they lay on the wheel or moved without intention along the dials and buttons of the dashboard.

He strained, pushed energetically, puffing as if he were about some honest task. But, later, when they were moving, she felt better, felt as if they had escaped and were now safe.

"I can't really believe it's happening," she murmured, as if to herself.

"No. Nor can I."

"He is . . . he's really in there? In that trunk?"

"Oh, yes."

After that they drove in silence, watching the black road lead them out of the houses and the wire fences and the pollarded trees into the green ease of fields and heath and untrimmed hedges.

At last Hassan said, "It was so easy."

"Easy!" She glanced sideways, feeling for the first time afraid of him. The man she sat beside was a murderer; she thought this word, wondering at its meaning. Understanding how the world would think of him, she felt overcome despite herself by a kind of warmth, a sense that in some way she would have to protect him from wrath and retribution.

He said, "It was as though I had nothing to do with it. I was hardly there—or just watching; watching, that is all. My hands moved, they moved here and there . . . Then he was dead."

She said nothing, having nothing to say, but instead swung the wheel, turned the car into the swoops and bends of a narrow, high-hedged lane.

Hassan said, "There is a sense in which I feel free now."

"Free?" She stared through the windscreen, licked dry lips. She hardly understood the conversation.

"It is a paradox; I realise that," he muttered.

"Because he was one of those who gave you your orders?"

"Oh, that . . ." He said this without interest. "No . . . or, yes, partly . . . But I moved as if I was automatic. Yet I feel free. What I did I could not stop, did not order, had no means of controlling—yet I feel let out of prison. What held me? What let me go?"

Laura, concentrating on their route, was no longer listening to him; and, indeed, he had stopped speaking to her, his low voice introspective, puzzled, meant only for his own clarification. He sat well back in his seat, frowning, not looking at the froth of leaves that whirled past the window, but staring down at his own tranquil feet.

"Here," Laura sharply said. She stopped the car, shut off the engine. Beyond the open window, the countryside hummed and twittered, laced with the clear song of bird and insect. Hassan slowly got out of the car, then turned, looked down at the unmoving Laura.

"Well?"

"Through the gate there," she said, glancing away from him. "On the right there's a ridge. Then, beyond that, there's water—an old gravel pit."

"Deep?"

"Yes. Very deep."

"You know it?"

"I lived here, near here; until I was eighteen."

"So there are houses?"

"Very few. And at this time, on a weekday, there wouldn't be many who . . ."

She let her voice drop and fade, then sat without moving. I played here as a child, she thought, but games get serious, the rules change . . . Not letting herself listen, she heard nevertheless the heavy scraping of the trunk, then the soft smack of its landing on the turf. On the edge of vision, Hassan's shadow passed, gigantically hump-backed as he bowed under the weight of what he carried. She bent slowly forward, rested her forehead on the wheel as though she had suddenly become overwhelmingly tired.

Hassan stumbled over the uneven ground, climbed the low ridge before him. At the top he halted, panting, feeling despite everything slightly absurd at standing thus laden on a deserted skyline.

59

Below him, black water lay between steep, carved banks. To his right stood a clump of bushes. He nodded, moved towards these. There, hidden by a mesh of leaves, he finally opened the trunk. Silver hair, sallow skin, below the nose the black of caked blood. Hassan stared, feeling himself once more in the grip of horror.

It is mine, he thought; I own this, having made it. It was a man, but I altered its condition and now it is this. But such conclusions were only cerebral, a thin film to cover fear. He bit his lip, hesitating; then, with eyes shut, bent and lifted the body. At the touch of this skin on his he thought for a moment he would vomit, but action brought cure; in a moment he was half-running through the trailing branches, carrying the dead man towards the water.

At the edge of the gravel pit he dropped the body. Sprawled in this way at his feet, it suddenly seemed less than real. It could never have been alive—the sense of freedom once more overwhelmed him. Despite himself, he gave a swift and nervous giggle. Hurrying, he scurried along the bank, collecting stones to fill the dead man's pockets.

Somewhere nearby, a girl laughed.

Hassan stood, stooped above pebbles, no less stone than they. Then, slowly, he turned; his terror-stricken heartbeat possessed the world. It was as if the whole landscape waxed and waned to his blood's rhythm.

Above the ridge a head appeared. Dark, this, a sort of ball. Hair, wind-ruffled; someone on the further slope, his back to the water, standing, watching something out of sight. And again a girl laughed.

Watching, then, a girl, Hassan thought. A young man, a girl; two people, out together, running, the ridge their target, the man outstripping the girl, turning to taunt her perhaps, or to wait, embrace her as she approached him . . .

Hassan threw himself to the ground beside his own unmoving partner. Over the head, staring eyes, he threw a handkerchief.

"Come on, slowcoach," the young man's voice called, his teasing tones floating on the easy wind.

Hassan bent the dead man's arm, forcing its stiffening joints and muscles into place under the head. Then he lay back, only his parted lips and shallow breathing witnessing to his fear.

Laughing, the dark-haired young man came into sight, running hand-in-hand with a tall, long-striding girl.

"A pond!" she shouted, as though surprised by the very fact of water.

Hassan sat up, turned. The movement caught the couple's attention and they slowed. Hassan put a finger across his lips, silently indicated the unmoving form beside him. The young man nodded, smiled, began with exaggerated caution to tip-toe over the grass. The girl copied him; with high and careful strides they moved along the slope. In a moment they burst once more into laughter, looked back once, answered Hassan's easy wave with one of their own, then had run out of sight.

Hassan stood, picked up the body, heavier now with its burial weight of stone. He walked to the edge of the pit. Below him the small cliff fell into the darkness of deep water. A sheen of silver wavelets covered this. Hassan hesitated, glanced left and right, then abruptly bowing, launched the body into oblivion.

The splash was muted. Clothes flared with air, bubbled, then collapsed. Limbs spread; thus broadly across the water, the body floated.

"Sink!" Hassan whispered. "There are gods, there is life . . . Sink!"

Slowly the shoes drifted into darkness. Half the body drooped, falling away towards invisibility. Water closed upon it. For a moment, like a trapped moon, the silver of hair repeated light. Then the surface evened, the tiny wavelets covered it as if in happiness, they shimmered above the black and secret depths. Hassan straightened; he could feel the tension leave the muscles of his face. His skin felt cold as the small wind dried the sweat of his terror. He turned, stumbled across grass, through bushes, his feet slipping as he scrambled to the ridge top and out of sight.

A gate slammed, then a car door. An engine revved. There was the whine of a slipping tyre, the high noise of an engine accelerating too rapidly. Then this faded. Insect and bird owned the countryside's interruptions.

Somewhere a man called, a girl answered.

"They've gone."

"Even the sleeper?"

"Both."

"He woke quickly."

"I expect it was us."

They sat side by side; they looked out over the simple beauty of pond and grass and hillside.

"Peaceful," she said, sighing.

"Yes," he murmured and, stretching out, pulled her to him.

"No," she murmured, bending into his kisses, muscles already softening for his caresses. "No. They might came back."

"They won't come back," he said, slowly stroking her thigh. Lengthening miles away, Hassan cried, "It's over. As easy as that. I have thought of the man so often—now it is over."

"And it was easy," Laura said, not without some bitterness in her voice.

"Yes. And simple. I had not realised the logic of violence. Do you see the simplicity? An action leads to a consequence. It has a curious clarity."

"You used to hate it."

"Yes. Perhaps it was that clarity I hated—the world is muddled and all clarity is a deception."

"So you haven't changed?"

"No," Hassan said with conviction. "No. I am the same. But this time I had need of violence; it was a clear situation and clarity provided the answer. All the same, I do not like this sort of situation, this sort of clarity."

She glanced at him, then back at the unwinding road. "Still, you said it was easy."

"Yes," he agreed thoughtfully. "Easy. I had imagined that there would be a block, that I would have to fight myself. But my hands moved here, then there . . . I had no chance to be critical, to ask myself what I was doing. Action solved all these complications of introspection. Everything was automatic; there was no block. So it was easy."

"This relieved you?"

"Surprised. I was surprised." His voice fell, he whispered. "Yes. Surprised, that was it. It was so quick, so strange, so different from what I had supposed . . . from what I had supposed I was."

After this he said no more until she stopped the car outside the house where he lived. Even then he sat, unmoving, shocked now, staring ahead of him.

"Well?"

He turned, looked at her. His eyes were wide, very black.

"You must come up," he said. "I have to have someone there. Just for a moment, for an hour or so . . ."

"All right," she said.

They walked without speaking up to the second floor. Moving slowly, they seemed as if infinitely weary; heavy-limbed, they climbed each step with a renewed effort, their heads hung, their shoulders were bowed as though under some weight, as though they carried physically the weight of that dead and sunken body.

"My room," Hassan said, and led Laura along the bright corridor. He shut the door behind them, then leaned against it, saying nothing, not looking up. After a moment, still not meeting her eyes, he stepped nearer her; his hands grasped her shoulders and held, tightly. They stood like this for a long time, unable to move again, or speak; it was as if witchcraft had transfixed them. Then, slowly, Hassan pulled her nearer. Trembling, she allowed this, shuffling to the pressure of his hands.

Hassan breathed deeply for a moment, then bent, buried his face in the warm curve of her neck and shoulder. He began to stroke her back, his hands moving in slow, circular caresses. After a while he stood straighter, put one arm firmly about her, led her silently to the bed. They sat down side by side.

"I don't know," she muttered. It was as if she were sullen. "I don't know."

But he was beyond words. He took her far shoulder, pulled her down, rolled as she fell back so that he lay with one leg between hers.

"But this," she said, "this, now . . ."

He did not hear. He needed warmth, comfort, oblivion. His right hand whisked along her thigh, found the stretched skin, the smoothness. His tongue fought hers, then stretched about her mouth until she felt already filled, already possessed. Panting, she stretched her head back until her eyes were shadowed by the disarranged waves of her hair. Her wide thighs flexed and flung; with a soft shock of noise, her right shoe fell to the carpet.

Abruptly Hassan lifted his weight off her, looked down.

"Well?" he asked. "Well? Well?"

She groaned, irresolute; his hand moved down the curve of her belly, his fingers softly probed.

63

"Yes," she said. "Yes, of course, now." But her voice was unsteady, as if she were about to sob.

"Then undress," Hassan demanded. There was an edge to the words, some hint of fury. He watched as she sat up, slipped her dress off her shoulders, then stood to let it drop to the floor. She hesitated, looking at him. His face was immobile; his dark eyes gleamed. Swiftly she finished undressing then stood naked and curiously helpless in the room's centre.

"You still love me," Hassan said.

"Yes."

"I dream about your body. I have dreamed about it all these months; there, and since I came back. All the time."

He leaned forward and, with the tips of his fingers, touched her left breast, watched the sudden blood lift the nipple, then ran his hand across and down her body, the movement slow, the fingers trembling: he was relearning a lesson he had thought forever to be forgotten. Suddenly he laughed, leaning away from her, his face given over to happiness.

"You!" he cried. "After all!"

And in a moment he was standing, flinging shirt and trousers and underclothes across the calm room like an out-of-place, out-of-season snowstorm. He caught her as she knelt half in and half out of the sheets; skin to skin they rolled across the white bed, his hands in and about her like fire, until she felt heat like some enormous balloon envelop her, snatch out of the normal dimensions of her life into planes and spaces of tension and desire that she had never experienced before. She heard herself howl, delight wilder than pain snatching her control. Then his body pinioned her and world and time contracted; then exploded, hotter than furnaces.

"Oh, that," she sobbed, weeping now, holding him tightly to her, happy in her spread flesh and the tension lifted. "That, that . . . I've waited so long, wound up, winding up, a turn every time I saw you or thought of you or remembered . . . That's cut all those months out of my life, all that wasted time."

He moved away from her, rolled to lie on his back, smiled sweetly at the ceiling. He said nothing.

"I must go." She sat up, stretched. He watched, quite coldly, the lift of her breasts, then the curve of back and buttock as she climbed out of bed.

Later, in pale blue briefs, she said, holding high a slip, "But you'll be in danger now," and stood, suddenly realising again all that had happened. "They'll come after you now," not moving, stricken by fear.

"Yes," he said. "They will wait for his report. But if he has not told them where I am, they will not be able to find me."

"They've my address."

"Then I must avoid it."

"But I can't always come here. Besides . . ."

He laughed, stretching too, then sitting up.

"Then I must come to you. Is there no other door?"

"The back door? But how? . . ."

"What is at the end of the garden?"

"Yes. A lane. There's a fence . . ."

"High?"

"No. In any case, I could take out one or two of the palings."

"You see!"

"But if they're looking . . ."

He got out of the bed, stood naked where she had stood, in the centre of the room. Without his clothes he no longer seemed plump; muscles moved in his shoulders and his chest was very deep.

"Eventually they will find me," he said. "Then there must be new decisions; we will have to think about all that. But in the meantime . . ." he moved to her, kissed her deeply, ". . . in the meantime, there is the meantime."

.   .   .

In the narrow hall, Martin danced, his arms stretched wide, his knees pumping up and down, high as a wing three-quarter's. As he whirled, he accompanied himself with a series of emphatic, atonal "pom-pom-pom" sounds. Blinking away the remains of sleep, Hassan came down the corridor.

"What is the time?" he asked.

"Tra-la, tra-la, tra-la, pom-POM!" Martin called and, massively reaching forward, took Hassan by the shoulders and hurled him too into the careless orbits of his dance.

"But why? . . ." Hassan began, then twirled, obedient to Martin's muscular insistence.

Martin shouted, "They've called me! They've called me."

"They?"

"I'm to be interviewed."

"You are called?"

"The first selection!"

"An interview? With whom?"

"It means they've done the first picking."

"Oh! Selected, picked out . . ."

"The competition? Yes, of course . . ."

Once more trapped by large Martin, Hassan swung about the hall.

"It means there's a short list," Martin explained. "It means I'm on it. It means they've picked out the few."

"A short list."

"The talented few."

Again Martin hurled himself upon Hassan; together they tramped to and fro, Hassan now and then clapping Martin on the shoulder or the arm by way of congratulation. Martin yelled out the uneasy harmonies and rhythms of his happiness, grabbed Hassan's wrists, swung him light-footed towards the tall front door. Which slowly opened.

"The dance is interesting, but I don't much care for the music," Ricky murmured, looking at them.

"Short list," Hassan cried.

"No less!" Martin added.

"Oh?" Ricky closed the door, turned with an expression of polite fatigue on her face.

Martin said, "The competition, Sablecombe—the Civic Centre."

"Ah. That short list."

"It is marvellous," Hassan said, fervently determined on admiration.

"It is," Ricky agreed, and went into the sitting room.

And later. "Why?" Martin asked her.

"Why what?"

Martin hesitated, leaning back with exaggerated casualness against the deep back of the black couch. Then, with a diffident shrug, he said, "You were so unenthusiastic . . ."

"Unlike, for instance, Hassan?"

"Hassan?"

Involuntarily, Martin glanced at the sitting room door, but all remained closed, silent, cordoning off Hassan within his private four walls; the deep fears and desires of which Martin knew nothing were contained in the coiled brain, the dark head careless in sleep, restless on the long pillow.

Ricky said, "He won't disturb us."

"No."

"He was enthusiastic."

"Yes. He was."

"Then perhaps that should have been enough."

Martin frowned, watched her as she turned abruptly away, with swift movements took, then lit, a cigarette.

She said, "You called me, after all. You said you had news to tell me."

"Wasn't it true?"

She swung round. "But you'd told it. The party was already on. I came in and suddenly saw you—closed circle, all necessary connections made. . ."

"Not all. In any case, you're saying that what I had to say should have been exclusively for you, that I should have kept . . ."

"Yes! Why not? Kept it till I came. Told no one before me. Yes. You should have—it should have been like that."

Martin suddenly sat forward, reached for her. "You're jealous of him," he said. "You're jealous of Hassan."

She took a curt step to take herself out of his reach. "What's my place in your life?" she asked.

"There's love, after all."

"Yes. Love." She nodded, frowning a little. "All the same, he does the housework, helps with the rent, is the first to be told good news—all that adds up to a place, some niche near the centre of things . . ."

Martin suddenly stood up. "But this is ridiculous. Near the centre—you're at the centre of things, however near he might be. You are the centre of things, for Christ's sake."

"No. I'm nowhere, really. A lay, when you or I feel the time's right. But London's the easiest town in the world for making women. God knows you wouldn't go short of that if I walked out."

"But a lay, the one-night stand—it's not what you and I . . ."

"It's sex, without direction. Soon it'll have no motive but itself. That's nothing."

"The same argument, then?"

"You and your Bohemian pretensions." She had turned, was sending words through bared teeth as if, snarling now, she might at any moment bite. "The beatnik thing, the sad and sagging bourgeois hippie. Don't you realise yet that no one's playing those games any more? Even the real artists have given those up. I want to be wife, I want to be mother, I want to have place and location and status. Oh, yes; status—why not? This endless, ageless, bloody teen-ager bit . . . I'm sick of that. We spend time together, hours and hours together—why not the whole time, why not the permanent arrangement?"

"You talk about it as if it's directed at you."

"Why not? Why not permanency?"

Martin looked at her in silence, then turned away, walked to the window, looked across cool summer.

"I'm no one, that's why," he said in a low voice.

"No one?"

"Things to be done, faces to be worn, a place to be dug. If the world's a battlefield, where's my fox-hole? Rank and location, that's what I lack. Can't you see that? To marry, just in the skin I stand up in . . ."

"You mean it's honour? The world's recognition? Marriage bells on condition you've built the belfry they hang in?"

"Built myself. There are things I want, and things I want to do. I need to build myself, to be consistent with the man I think I am or want to be. There are ambitions, there's a kind of acceptance . . . No, it's not honour, it's not being wanted or feted or praised. It's becoming who I might be. It's realising the potential. Or realising that there isn't any."

"And being content with that? If there should be none, if it all turns out dreams—being able to accept that?"

"If it were to be proved; yes."

She waited a moment, then walked nearer him, gentler now. "And you won't think I might help with that? Another pair of hands to set the bricks in their ambitious courses?"

He faced her. "I want to be whole. I'm not completed. I can't venture into something that's labelled 'permanency' unless I feel I'm whole. Healed of youth and, all right, dreams; healed of

68

dreams."

"Love heals. My love would."

"Does," he murmured. "Does already. That wound . . . But there are others."

"Wounds?"

"It feels like that. Yes."

They stood on opposite ends of a green rug. They watched each other for lies or evasion. Then she smiled, half shrugged, took the two steps that brought her into his embrace.

PART THREE

*If once a man indulges himself in
murder, very soon he comes to
think little of robbing; and from
robbing he comes next to drinking
and sabbath-breaking, and from
that to incivility and procrastination.*
                                    De Quincey

Hassan lay, drowsily stretched, in his broad bed. Outside the window, summer dressed the trees in heavy leaves, the sky with light. Birds fenced their territories with song. Like peasants grateful for the endless largesse of a benevolent lord, flowers turned towards the sun.

Death lay sprawled across Hassan's memory. Restlessly, he moved his head; but within his skull the other, dead skull lay, the grey hair of its scalp bright on the carpet, then feebly bright in dark water, descending. His hands moved in that other time, dealing murder. Laura heard him, not understanding what she heard, then drove him and his twisted corpse to burial: the grey hair, feebly bright, sank into dark water. Dead too, his mother walked between the uniforms, her face as always turned back, turned to speak, to call through the indestructible silence some last word of instruction and love. And Laura spoke, listened, drove; then lay, opened by desire, awaiting possession, awaiting the being possessed . . . But, as often in the changing weeks, her face fell away, its writhing lips, still grasping at sensation, settling in corrupt promise on Ricky's features instead; it was Ricky who lay for love, Ricky who cried her joy in the arena of Hassan's mind.

He turned, then turned again; finally sat up. It was still early. On the lawn, out of sight below the window, a thrush yelled hunger or challenge. Hassan got up, rubbed with both hands his black disordered hair. From behind the door he took a brown and orange robe, then walked to the kitchen.

Kettle in hand, he turned at a sound. In the doorway, halted by astonishment, stood Ricky. She wore a short, white night-shirt. Light fell through it, seemed as if meshed between cloth and skin. Hassan stared at her, at the deep breasts, the white circle of belly, the fall of hip and thigh, the dark-brown pubic triangle. Then the girl had stepped back and, with a sweep of her hand, had slammed shut the door. For a long time Hassan, alone, stood in the silent kitchen. In the kettle he held the water rustled as it shifted to and fro; his hand was trembling, his whole body was shuddering, racked as if he had suddenly contracted a fever. Then, soberly, his face closed as if with grief, he began to make his breakfast.

Carefully chewing toast, he heard the front door bang shut; in a moment, Martin came heavy-footed into the kitchen.

"Early," he muttered.

"Yes," Hassan agreed. He sat tensely, not looking at Martin. "Ricky has left?" he asked.

"Seemed, yes, rather keen to get off." Martin looked blankly about him as if searching for reasons, then sat down.

Pouring coffee, Hassan said, "Don't you think you ought to marry her?"

"Ought?" Eyes on his cup, Martin offered no more than a weak imitation of outrage. "That's no word. And don't you bloody start."

"She feels it, then? She asks you?"

"Sometimes. Too often. It's unsettling."

"I cannot see why you do not."

"Self-respect."

"Yours?"

"Of course."

"Yes, Naturally."

Martin stared at him over the cup's rim. "All right—if you're so keen on the institution, why aren't you married?"

"Because she is married already."

"This woman? The one who calls you Osman?"

"Yes. Laura."

"Laura. And she's married?"

"I went away very suddenly. I was away for over a year. My circumstances made writing letters a little difficult . . ."

"Prison?" Martin laughed briefly.

"No. But a course, a very demanding and absorbing course of training. So that when I came back . . ."

"Well, that's not an unusual story."

"I did not choose it. It chose me."

"No, I'm sorry. That was flippant."

Both drank coffee, Martin contrite after his lack of concern, Hassan slowly burgeoning into relief at Ricky's having said nothing about her near-naked encounter with him.

"Tell you what," Martin said abruptly, "if everything goes reasonably well in the competition, Ricky and I'll be going to the Pennines for a holiday."

"The Pennines?"

"Well, Peak District. Derbyshire. Why don't you come with Laura?"

"A holiday? But if you want to be together . . ."

"There's no one else there. It's big enough to keep separate. A big old house. If she can get away . . ."

"I will ask her."

"Because otherwise you'd be alone, womanless, and that's no fun. Long dark nights, once you go out of London. And as an architect, I approve of symmetry—two men, two birds: the proportions please me."

Hassan smiled, a little warily. "As long as Ricky's proportions continue to appeal a little more than Laura's . . ."

Martin laughed, stood up. "Wife-swapping on the backbone of England? I expect they do it all the time up there."

"The British have always worked hard at their hobbies."

Both laughed. Martin carried cups and plates, glanced at the kitchen clock.

Hassan said, "At what stage is the competition?"

"Five of us are left—five or six, I think. I have to go and expound at some point, explain to the committee what they're looking at."

"It will mean a great deal, doing well?"

"My life. More and more of doing what I want, less and less of working like a hack over other people's ideas. That self-respect I was talking about. A place in the sun."

"Marriage?"

Martin grinned. "Maybe," he said. He glanced once more at the clock. "Work time," he added, then went out.

Hassan stood by the sink. His head drooped, his shoulders sagged. He looked like a man beyond weariness, at the point of collapse.

.   .   .

She stood in the same attitude and the same place as she had when, three days before, she had been in her nightdress. Hassan, turning amid the rising scent of coffee from the bubbling percolator, remained in the twisted posture of one arrested awkwardly in mid-movement. He and Ricky stared at each other; they had not met since then.

"Martin isn't here?" she said.

"No. Not yet."

She nodded, came into the kitchen, sat at the narrow, plastic-covered table.

"Coffee?"

"Yes," she said. "Thanks."

He took the coffee off the stove and they waited while it dripped through, both watching the percolator now as if they expected it to do something preternatural, extraordinary; fly, perhaps, or speak.

In a low voice, Hassan said, "You should make Martin marry you."

Astonished, she jerked back in her chair. Out of her suddenly pale face her eyes stared at him, their green irises enormous.

"Is it your business?"

"You are my friends. I see you."

"There's nothing that . . . What Martin and I have to work out, we'll work out together. And alone."

"Yes." Hassan nodded slowly, thoughtfully. "The coffee's ready," he said, and poured a cup for her.

Silently, they drank, their eyes not meeting.

"I do not think he will marry you," Hassan said softly after a while.

"Won't?" Her voice trembled, perhaps with anger.

"In my country, women are married at fourteen."

"In your country!" She almost shouted this. "Yes, arranged by a couple of old crones, and dished out four to a man."

"That is changing. I think you should marry."

"Oh, I'll marry. Martin and I—we'll come to that."

"If not? . . ."

"What?"

"It might go on like this; you might live like this for years."

"Why don't you leave it alone? All this, the subject?"

"How long, for instance, have you lived like this already?"

"The years that . . . But we arranged it; we have will, our own intentions. There's no need for you to play broker." She pushed her cup away, the half-empty coffee slipping in black tongues over the rim and into the saucer. With a violent movement, she got to her feet.

Hassan said, "There are others."

"Others? What others?"

"Those who see you, who meet you. Who see you."

"Like you?"

"For example."

"You!" She stood very straight beside the table. Without words in her astonishment, she stared at him, shaking her head from side to side in an endless, amazed negative.

"For example, I. An example. There is money, a degree; there will be work. And a place more exotic than this, warmer, more beautiful. I have a house, gardens; there are mountains to be seen from some of the windows, the sea from others . . ."

"You! But that's not serious. Is that what this was about, this conversation? 'You are my friends'—then this? Do you really imagine . . . But you aren't a man at all, in my catalogue. What are you? You potter in the kitchen, you lie in your room . . . There's this story of a thesis, but I don't believe that; I don't think there's a thesis. You and your housework and your masochistic little games of servant and master—you're no man for a woman, a woman like me. Good God, it's not me you want, it's Martin!"

Pale-faced, bending awkwardly forward, she began a high-pitched, hysterical laugh. From under her brows her wild eyes watched him.

He sat at the kitchen table, not looking at her, silent and staring straight ahead. Once, a muscle beside his mouth jumped, then jumped again.

"You do not really know me," he said, evenly. "You have no idea of what I can do."

Once more, and briefly, they faced each other; then she had whirled, gone out, the door closing softly behind her.

Still without expression he turned to the sink, took the cups and saucers and spoons, began to wash them. Behind him he heard the door open again.

"I'm sorry," she said. "It's a sore place—a trampled battleground, this notion of marriage."

He did not turn round. "It is my fault. It is, of course, nothing

77

to do with me."

"I'm tired—there's the competition, that he's on the short list: because if he wins it, I mean . . ."

He had still not faced her and her voice trailed away. She nodded at his back, saying no more.

"It is my fault," he said again. "It is ridiculous of me to interfere. Or to suggest alternatives."

"No, that was . . . I had no business to . . ."

"Ridiculous!" Now he turned. His face was pale, almost, she thought, green. His black eyes glittered like chips of coal. "It was absurd. I realise how it must have seemed to you."

With an effort, she murmured, "It was a compliment—and sweet . . ."

"Please do not consider it again. Or think of it. Ever!"

"I shouldn't have said . . ."

His lips thinned and lifted; his white teeth were suddenly revealed in a vulpine sneer. "Let us consider it a moment of mutual weakness, then." His voice was harsh. She saw his right hand twitch, half-lift, then fall to his side. "A moment of sentimental confusion. A sort of involuntary clowning."

He walked past her, his sneer now modified into the politeness of a fixed and unreal smile.

"Please," she said. She put her left hand on his sleeve. For a moment he hesitated; she felt under the cloth the roll and tensions of muscles.

"It is, of course, already forgotten," he muttered, in his voice the suggestion that this was more question than statement. Then he had stepped into the corridor.

A moment or so later she heard him go out of the apartment.

.   .   .

Hassan sat in lamplight, his eyes closed. To his right, upright and watching him, Laura sat in an armchair. In her right hand she turned a whiskey glass round and round, the gesture slow and reflective rather than nervous.

"Do you remember that holiday in Wales?" she asked.

Hassan nodded, not smiling. "The Gower—those beaches. And then Tenby. And afterwards the mountains . . ."

"Cader Idris."

"And rain."

Suddenly they both laughed, then as abruptly stopped.

Hassan said, "And now?"

"It's different."

"Do you remember when the car broke down?"

"And that old woman? . . ."

"Yes. Called us in and we ran across the rain and she had tea and welsh-cakes . . ."

"And embroidered texts on the wall. And all that polished furniture . . ."

"She's still there. She—others like her."

Laura shook her head. "No. It's different now. You know it is."

She walked to a long sideboard, refilled her glass, dropped ice into the whiskey, sat down again.

"I want a future," Hassan said in a low voice. "There is no way I can accommodate to the life I live now. We have a past—memories that we have in common. We are together now; often together. It seems silly that we may not think about a future."

"All that was changed. You went away."

"I told you about that."

"Too late."

"You mean, there is all this—all this is the future for you? You already live in your future and this is it? Money, a travelling husband, me for a lover—is that the shape it will be?"

Laura drank, shook her head again. "No. But there are obligations, aren't there? I can't just take a man to cover a gap in my life—not to marry him, make him set up a home and put me in it and when he's done all that, get up and leave him because there's a past come back to claim me."

"And love?"

She said nothing, but swallowed what was in her glass, then held it out to him. "Could you?"

He took it, walked to the sideboard, poured a little, held it up.

"That is the last of it."

"No more than that?"

"No more."

He brought her the glass and she nodded at it, smiled at him, sipped.

"Will you get drunk, then?" he asked.

"No. But there's no rule that says you can't put a bandage on a wound, is there?"

"There are no rules of any sort. That is why I say there is a future."

"Don't talk of it. For the moment let it go. Can't you? Can't you let things happen . . . go on happening, as they are now?"

"It is not enough. Not enough."

He leaned back and once more closed his eyes. It was as if the landscape he carried within him gave him more comfort than this room he sat in, this woman with whom he sat.

"Why not? Why not enough?"

"I need more. That is the simplest answer. It is not enough because I need more."

"But if I say that there can be no more?"

"Then I must accept what there is, while needing what will not be given."

"Why must you have more?"

"Because when I was a child I had a home, and when I was a student I had my career and now I am a man and I have nothing. I must have a shape to my life, and the shape needs a centre and you are what should be that centre. My life should be built about you; that is what my emotions tell me."

She shook her head again, unable to speak. She could feel tears heavy under her eyelids.

"Too late," she murmured. "Really, it has to be . . ."

"Yes. For the moment. But perhaps you will learn to need me."

But his voice was suddenly dull, dispirited.

Laura said, "You're sure there was no more whiskey?"

He stood up, abruptly brisk.

"I will get you more."

"No, Osman, really . . ."

"He is to the left, the wine merchant?"

"Yes, left—but you'll be careful?"

"The garden, the fence, the lane—then left to the off-licence."

"Will they be open?"

Hassan glanced at his watch. "Just," he said; then walked quickly from the room.

In the doorway of the off-licence, the owner was stretched like a spider across light, arms splayed as he reached for the high blind.

Hassan knocked on the glass. The man inside, still stretching up, looked at him, shook his head, began to pull the blind down.

Hassan pushed, heaved the door open an inch or two. The owner stepped back, thrust his head forward, said, "What the hell are you doing?"

Hassan stood inside the door. "My girl friend would like a bottle of whiskey."

"Should have thought of it sooner, then, shouldn't she!"

"Perhaps. But she has . . . she has a pain . . ."

"Well, I'd get a doctor. Pushing and shoving your way in here . . ."

"Please. If you want to charge me extra . . ."

"Home, that's all I want. Now get out."

"The whiskey, please."

"Look, we're closed. Right? You understand that? Closed! I want to go home and I've closed the shop and so there's no whiskey. All right?"

Hassan stared at the man. Outside, the street was silent, tense under the brittle darkness of summer.

He said, "You could have given me the bottle and I would have paid you. You could have been on your way home by now."

"Don't tell me how to run my business. I've shut the shop and you're bloody trespassing. Now get on out of it!"

He stepped nearer Hassan, his mouth set and stubborn. Hassan did not move. The two men watched each other, each conscious of wills forcefully tangling. It was the owner who broke first. With a sudden shout, a bubbling in the throat as if breath had suddenly left him, he thrust out his right hand to push Hassan through the door.

Hassan brought his hands together like the closing jaw of a vice. The man screamed, looking down in sudden stupidity at his dangling hand and the pain of crushed bones. Hassan, his face serene, stepped nearer. His hands stabbed, then cut; fingers, then blade of palm, bit deep into flesh. Blood fell into sight, black in the neon-lit shop. The owner dropped to his knees. His eyes, bright with amazement, stared briefly up at Hassan; then glazed. The crash as he fell sideways seemed very loud.

"Now you understand," Hassan said, steadily. He was not sure to whom he spoke. "Now you know."

He stared down at the still, collapsed man. Slowly, in sudden starts, he began to shiver. He went down on one knee, touched the man's shoulder, then let his hands flutter across the chest towards the heart. There was no sound, no steady contracting rhythm. Hassan stood, slammed shut the door, let down the blind, then bent over the shop's owner—ex-owner—again. Blank eyes stared past him at the mottled ceiling. Letting out a long unsteady sigh, Hassan stood up. For a moment he did not move, looking left and right as if uncertain where he was. Then he turned, ran from the shop, hearing the door crash to behind him, to cut him off from this new evidence of what he had become.

"It was shut," he said as he stepped back into the lights and comfort of Laura's sitting room.

Laura laughed. "I thought it would be. It was very gallant of you to go. But I found some vodka—that'll see me through."

"You mean, you did not really need it?"

"That's right. I'm sorry. Silly, isn't it."

Hassan nodded, began to laugh—a dry, harsh laugh, like a consumptive's cough. "Yes. Silly."

Laughing too, Laura reached for his hand, pulled him towards her. Looking up at him, she sobered. He watched her eyes darken, watched the faint bewilderment creep into them. He glanced away. She had noticed his perturbation, but now misinterpreted it.

"We haven't talked about it," she said. "We carry on as if nothing has happened—but there was that . . . that trunk . . ."

"I know."

He watched the light on the disappearing head, the fading silver lost in water; but over that, obscuring it, now lay the sprawled figure of the man he had just killed.

"Killed!" he muttered. "Killed!"

She nodded, looked down. Her hand tightened about his wrist. "A word, short, like that—or 'death'. That's the word . . . I can't grasp it, I can't really take it in. And that you, I mean . . . that you could have done it—or even what 'it' is . . . And then that I helped you, helped with that—killing, death . . ."

"I don't understand it," Hassan said. He moved away from her, looked down at his hands, tensed his fingers for a moment, then relaxed, let his arms drop. "I don't understand. My hands move, they just go up, down, across; they are alone, they seem to govern themselves . . . But that cannot be the truth. They are no different from what they were before, from anyone else's hands. But they are trained, now; the moves are in their nerves, in their muscles, in my arms and shoulders and spine, like animals, like some pack of wolves waiting to be let out . . ."

"Again?"

"What?"

"Do you think it might happen again?"

The question entwined him like a net. He did not look at her, needing to struggle against its strands.

"I do not know," he murmured. "If there is provocation or . . ."

"Provocation?"

"Yes."

"Of what sort?"

"If someone . . . if there should be a situation . . ."

"Another of them, you mean? Another of their people?"

"Yes. Another of them."

"You should go away."

"Perhaps."

But she crossed the room, held him fiercely. "No," she said. "We mightn't talk about it, but after what we've done . . . No. Don't leave me alone with it."

He kissed her, feeling the long warmth of her body against his, trying to press her into him as though her heat would keep him safe.

He said, "Look, there might be a chance of a holiday. There is a sort of invitation . . ."

"A holiday? With you?"

"In Derbyshire. A house, some old cottage. If it should be confirmed, would you be able to come?"

She frowned, then nodded. "He's away so often—why not? I could tell him some story—I've friends, after all. People I haven't visited since he and I were married. Yes, I could come with you."

"It would put a sort of distance of time between . . . all that's happened and the present we would be living in then. A sort of barrier."

In the distance there was the rise and fall of a siren; an ambulance, perhaps; or a police car.

"We'd have a little peace," she said. "Away from all this—from town, my husband, your dangers . . . Oh, yes, I'd love to come."

He kissed her again, his hands pulling her towards him. He could feel her thighs brush against his as she began her habitual swaying enticement. Warm, these; but he remembered that another woman had stayed distant.

"No," he said. "I must go."

"Go?"

"There are people, in the morning—something to do with rates . . ." But in the morning, perhaps, would be Ricky.

"Couldn't you stay? All the same—stay with me?"

"I have a headache, I need to get up early—no, I must go." Go where, he thought; remembering rejection.

She nodded, let him go.

"When will I see you?"

"I will telephone tomorrow, perhaps—I must arrange things."

He seemed like a man about to collapse, into fury, perhaps, or hysteria; his face was working, his eyes flicked to and fro as if he expected attack, the sudden intrusion of enemies.

"What's the matter?" she asked.

Within him, he seemed to sense a desert, a waste covered by the thin scream of endless winds. There was cold there, a tundra doomed to endless desolation.

"My head," he muttered. "A headache . . ."

But over desolation's horizon, like a great arctic sun, Ricky's face rose, contorted with contempt; it was her voice which sent out that withering wind. He put his palm flat on his forehead, as if to hold the bones of his skull in place. He felt taken over, properly possessed; as if the patterns and expectations of normality had been swept away, as if the psychic skin that kept a man from chaos had been breached.

He said, "I don't understand. Suddenly, there is a pain; such a curious pain . . ."

"If you're ill . . ."

"No. Not ill. But the world is turning; or changing—I don't understand . . ."

His hands were trembling now and there was sweat on his face. It was as if he were in terror. And perhaps I am, he

84

thought; I am afraid; I have held that back, I have behaved like a man with no death in his hands, but now that control has left me. I have no protection from the truth.

"I must go home," he said again.

"Do you have pills, aspirins?"

"Yes. I'll take some, go to bed."

"You could stay here—I'd look after you."

She smiled at him, but he shook his head. All he wanted now was darkness, silence, solitude. It seemed to him as if her face wavered, as if its planes and hollows moved unpredictably to and fro, shifting meaning and identity: it was as if her face were no more than a mask for Ricky's, as if her concern were no more than the false disguise of that other's contempt.

He tried to smile, muttered goodnights, then stumbled out into the warm, dark summer. For a long time Laura stood at her back door, islanded in light, straining to see and hear him, half expecting that, defeated, he would return.

But he, head down, walked under the stunted suburban trees, his eyes half shut as if to hold in misery.

Streets away, authority's sirens howled again.

.   .   .

Martin smoked, frowned as he took the cigarette from his mouth, said, "Not much longer now."

"How long?"

"Well, they've seen us, they've heard what we have to say; if they're any good as judges, they'll have a decision soon." He grinned, but like a condemned man. "In fact, in three days precisely."

"Three days!"

"So they've said."

They looked at each other, not knowing what to say, how to ease their mutual nervousness.

Finally Ricky smiled. "Try to forget it. There's nothing to be done."

"No. The work's finished—all that's left is the worry."

"Let me do that—you've done your bit."

He smiled. After a pause, he asked, "How much do you dislike Hassan?"

"Dislike?"

"Well, don't you?"

"I don't know that the word's 'dislike'. He makes me uncomfortable sometimes."

"You're jealous of him, that's all."

"Yes. In a way. But we've had that row. There's more than that." She hesitated, then said, "He fancies me, you see."

"Really?"

"Yes."

"He's said so?"

She shrugged. "In a sort of way."

Martin put his head back, gave a loud cry of laughter. "Wily, after all, then," he said. "Sly—creeping about while my back's turned . . ."

She shook her head. "No. He hasn't done anything, or said much. And maybe it isn't true. He always behaves very well."

"Good. Because—do you remember?—when he came we decided we'd ask him to come to Derbyshire with us . . ."

"No!"

"What?"

"You haven't asked him! You haven't put it to him, all bright and official?"

"Yes. He was talking about his woman, this Laura of his, and I said . . ."

"No!" Ricky stood up, her face tense with anger.

"But, darling, we agreed to it. We talked about it and thought it was a pretty good idea. We said . . ."

"I know what was said. But other things have been said since —enough to make you ask if I disliked him. Things like that have been said. And you shouldn't have invited him without finding out what I felt about it."

"But we . . ."

"What I felt about it now."

"No, it won't do! You admit he's done nothing. Simply because you're jealous . . . You say yourself he fancies you—why shouldn't I be jealous, for Christ's sake? He helps, he's quiet, he makes jokes . . ."

"He's changed since the beginning. But that isn't it."

"Changed?"

"Yes."

"How changed?"

86

"But that isn't it. It's a question of lives, of our lives and our being together. Is he going to share everything? Every place, every hour? I suppose you'll want him in the bloody bedroom next?"

"It's not me—what'll Laura think?"

"No. I don't want stupid jokes. Why can't we be alone? Are you scared of that—of our being alone? Do you need a chaperone? Are you afraid that if we go away together people might talk? My good name might be compromised, you might be forced to marry me by public opinion?"

"Now you're making the jokes."

"Those aren't jokes. I'm sick of it—you drag him with you like some dog, like a mascot . . ."

"I haven't dragged him anywhere."

"You arranged this! Not a word to me—you know how I feel, what I've said . . ."

"But we decided . . ."

"That was weeks and weeks ago. I wasn't very sure then. But I know now—and you knew I'd changed my mind. That's why you spoke to him first . . ."

"Oh, for heaven's sake, Ricky, this is all such a lot of bloody nonsense."

"All right, then. Will you tell him you've changed your mind?"

Martin set his chin, seemed at last as angry as she. "I won't be told who my friends are nor how I have to treat them!"

"All right. You go on your bloody holiday. You and your boyfriend . . . I hope you'll be happy."

"You know that's childish . . ."

"I've got wishes. I've got a right to be asked. I won't be walked over, trodden down."

"I don't like people who go back on their word! If something's arranged . . ."

"All right!" she screamed. "All right! All right!"

She slammed shut the door. He heard her run across the hall and slam the front door to behind her. Her feet clattered on the stairs; then silence seemed quite suddenly to reassert itself.

Martin stood, looking a little puzzled now, still staring at the shut door.

"What in hell? . . . I mean, what the hell got into her? If

87

she really can't stand him . . ."

In darkness, Hassan walked. His head was breached, a dam useless against the floods of night. It seemed as though the blackness swirled in and out, as if his skull, like an old hulk sodden with nightmares, was foundering now in obliterating tides. Ahead of him, someone walked. Closer, he saw it was a woman; it was Ricky. He began to pant, hurrying, a sweat as if of terror on his face. Ricky, frightened, turned to face who followed her: her face collapsed, fell into itself like a puffball—then reassembled, the features a stranger's, the mouth falling open in astonishment and fear.

Hassan passed by, trembling again. He had nearly put out his hand, taken that shoulder, said something, a word of greeting or attack; but had been mistaken.

"That would have been awkward," he muttered, and heard himself giggling. Then, silently, head down, he hurried without direction through the warm night. And again Ricky stood in the street, waiting for him it seemed—a Ricky built out of a twist of shadow, a projection of stone, a doorpost. Then her face was everywhere, falling like snow crystals from some unseen heaven of dream. Her mouth called silently from unlit windows, her face sneered at him from beyond yellow pools of lamplight, her voice called him, faintly, past the sound of wind-rustled leaves and the distant clatter of a goods yard.

"But I can't," he whispered. "I can't . . . All this isn't what . . . can't be stood, understood . . . I can't!"

On the blank pavement in this unknown suburb, he turned as if trapped, whirled as if about to dance, wept without sound.

While she herself, elsewhere, stood at a bus stop, still furious, upright, pale-faced, prosaically waiting but continuing her drama, nursing the warmth of her anger. She would go home, she would keep silence and distance about her like a moat, this Martin Prescott would learn that she was not to be treated like someone dumb, owned; like a slave.

"Like a slave!" she muttered, unconcerned with the nervous attention this aroused in those about her. "But I'm not that, not a slave." And she nodded vigorously to emphasise the point, speaking to the humbled Martin in her head.

In a telephone box, Hassan: his hand unsteadily leafing through a directory. Clumsily, on the back of a cigarette packet, he scribbled an address, then glanced at the notice on the wall which told him where he was. Finally, he dialled, asked for a taxi to pick him up.

Martin, meanwhile, marched solemnly up and down his long sitting room, his rage uncertain. Had he been wrong? But no, he had not; it had been she, who . . . All the same, he might have asked her what she felt. But he had asked her; and if he had not, had never even mentioned it, was she to dictate who his friends were, the pleasures of his holidays, the shape of his life? Yet who had that right, if not she?

"No rights!" he shouted and picked up an ashtray, hurled it at the wall. It struck heavily; paper tore, a thin avalanche of plaster rustled towards the carpet.

"Christ!" he yelled, in his uncertainty; perhaps it was more prayer than blasphemy. He walked swiftly to the door, went purposefully out. Then returned, not yet prepared to follow her.

"Why should I? Why should I run after her?"

He poured himself whiskey, threw himself long-legged into a chair, scowled into his glass for a moment, then drank. And at the moment of his glass's rising, Hassan bent over coins, steadied the trembling of his hand, paid off his taxi. On the other side of the road rose the red-brick and glass cliffs of an apartment block. Hassan slowly crossed the road. His teeth were chattering as if he were very cold, or suffering from fever, but he did not notice. He pushed through the high swing doors, glanced at what he had written on the cigarette packet, hesitated a moment, then took the lift. He got out on the third floor. He walked along a corridor, frowning at the numbered doors; then returned, ran down one flight of stairs, found the floor below, searched again.

Outside Number 15 he stopped. He stood without moving for a long time. Then, slowly, he raised his hand, set his pointed finger delicately on the bell-push.

The lights went out. Hassan, with a gasp, stepped back. But there was no sound, no sudden challenge or rush of running feet. He glanced at his watch; it was half past eleven.

"Time switch," he told himself. "That's all. Lights out!"

He felt that he would at any moment collapse into giggles; controlling himself he stepped forward once more, rang the bell. He waited; then rang again. No one replied. For a moment longer he hesitated; then, bending down, frowning in concentration, he began to apply what he had been taught to the simplicities of this lock.

Still furious, but consciously so, forcing anger, Ricky stepped off the bus, began to walk home. Had she not, after all, exaggerated? No; she was owed respect, equality. Martin had no right to face her with some *fait accompli*. All the same, she had been a little hysterical; it was true that he had mentioned it and that she had agreed. But that was time ago; since then she had changed her mind about Hassan—soft Hassan, turning softly from the housekeeping to ask her to marry him—and Martin had had no right to go back to the earlier plan without talking to her again. It was a question of principle. With face implacably set, she marched down the long, lamplit pavements.

With a crash Martin hammered the glass down on the table-top. He stood up, hesitated again, seemed about to sit down; then ran from the room. He had questions to ask, overtures, perhaps apologies, to make. Happy at decision, he ran down the stairs. In the empty flat behind him, a telephone rang for a while, stopped, rang again. At the wire's other end, Ricky listened to the forlorn double-tone of the ringing, then slammed the receiver on its cradle, stepped out of the telephone booth.

"He'll be drinking, then; laughing somewhere, refusing as always to . . ."

Her heels clattered against the pavement as she came round the last corner into the street where she lived. She crossed the road, pushed through swing doors—Hassan had passed through them almost exactly seventeen minutes before. She stepped into the lift, slammed the gate into place. Close by, Martin sat forward in his taxi, pointed a direction, glanced anxiously at street names.

Ricky stepped from the lift, shut its gate, then its wooden door, felt with her left hand, put on the corridor's time switch.

"Left, now—that's the street," Martin called through the glass partition, watched the driver nod and swing his wheel.

Ricky searched for her keys, fumbled for a moment, then opened the door. Her right hand stretched for light; but fingers met hers, a hand grasping out of darkness, settling about her wrist, pulling. She was flung forward, stumbling over the rug, nearly losing her footing. A bladed hand meant for her throat swept past her left temple; her attacker had expected her upright. In the corridor, the light went out.

"No," Ricky said, almost softly. Her breathing was constricted, her throat dry. I must scream, she thought; but it was beyond her strength. To her right she could hear her attacker panting, the sound high and rasping; he too was afraid.

"What do you want?" she asked.

The hand swept towards her again, but in the dark was out of distance. She stepped back; the unseen bulk of who was with her in this nightmare came closer. Falling backwards, she hit the wall beside the still-open door. A blow struck her on the right cheek and threw her to the left. And now she screamed, the shock releasing terror; screamed out into the corridor, all her force and body concentrating on this scream, every muscle contorted with the effort of producing it, yet not hearing it at all, not taking in the sound of it nor its echoes as they rolled down the building's stairwell; no longer even knowing what she was doing, what she was.

A foot kicked her, someone stepped on her hair as it lay loose across the doorway. Then there was a running down the corridor. Ricky, bending forward, began to sob, long, dry attempts at weeping that seemed like checked screams of pain.

The lift moaned, rising. On the stairs, swift feet. Neighbours opened doors. Down the corridor, the lift doors clashed. Light trapped Ricky, lying distraught at her own front door.

And Martin said, "What is it? What happened?"

"A scream," someone cried. "I heard a scream. It must have been . . ."

Held tightly, safely in strength she recognised, Ricky said unevenly, "Someone—he hit me . . . I don't know . . . He hit me, was waiting . . ."

"Did you see who?"

"Someone, hitting me—then he ran, he ran down the stairs . . ."

And Martin had gone again, running too, while one of the two teachers who lived next door wiped Ricky's bruised and bleeding cheek and the other brought the hot, sweet tea she was the only one with the presence of mind to make.

The swing doors faintly moved—still moved; Martin running, registered this; then was out in the night. Here, all was tranquillity, suburban peace; or menace, perhaps, each shadow an ambush. Martin stood still and listened. To the right came a scuffling, the sliding tread of running feet.

"You!" Martin called into the darkness. He ran again. At the first corner he glanced right, then left. Faint lights ribbed a long wooden fence with shadow. Nothing moved—then something. A shadow in shadow, a humped shape, in and out of lamplight's cone.

Martin ran again, his head down, not thinking about what murder he risked, about who might now be crouched in any dark place. The fence dropped away. Scaffolding rose, low dunes of bricks piled for the morning, concrete mixers black as monsters, the skeletal steeple of a crane. And a plank turned, a foot stepped into splashing mud; then into silence.

More quietly, slowly, Martin walked into this petrified jungle. Silence was like a web. He crept along planks, hid in the improvised caves left by the chances of construction, moving towards sound that always faded and finally died away. When he was alone on the building site, he knew it; the awareness straightened him. Suddenly he felt weak, knew the sweat cooling on his face. He sat down, put his head in his hands, waited for the feeling of nausea to pass. Then, slowly, he went back to the apartment building and Ricky.

He found her sitting, half-covered by a rug, smiling a little now, talking to one of the next-door teachers. Police came and went. Then he and Ricky were alone.

"Oh, I was frightened, so frightened."

She lay against his chest, trembling again, her face hidden.

"Did you think I'd come to wreak a terrible revenge?" he asked, his mocking tender.

She shook her head, then shrugged. "I don't know. Maybe your henchman—Hassan, or someone."

Holding each other, they laughed themselves into happiness.

.   .   .

"It's a question of murder, I'm afraid, ma'am."

"Murder?" Her heart contracted, convulsively tightened; then lay in her, diamond-hard, icy. "But it's so late . . ."

Laura in dressing gown stood in her tiled hall and looked up at the two men in pale mackintoshes, at the third man in uniform beyond.

"I'm sorry about that. But we have to ask at the houses closest by."

"It's near here?"

In her surprise she stared at them, her eyes rolling from one face to another. She felt the weight of fear slide off her; weakly she smiled, then turned, half-tottered towards the living room.

"Perhaps in here . . . If we sat in here . . ."

She fell heavily into a chair, rubbed a white hand across her forehead. Suddenly, she felt like laughing.

"You heard nothing, ma'am?"

"No. What should I? . . ."

"Perhaps shouting. Some sort of quarrel."

"No. Nothing. Where was? . . ."

"Someone assaulted Richards, the man who keeps the off-licence."

"Off-licence!"

"Yes. Why? Is there something that? . . ."

"Oh, no. It's just that I've been there—he's someone one knows."

"You weren't there tonight?"

"No."

"You know him well?"

"Well? No; it's just that . . . one goes there, you know. He keeps a shop and one uses it."

"Kept a shop."

"He was attacked, you say?"

"Beaten up; but scientifically. It was done by someone who's learned—ex-commando, someone like that."

"I'm sorry. I don't know anyone like that at all."

"No, ma'am. We didn't think you would. It's just to get the time. If you'd heard a shout, someone screaming . . ."

"No." She struggled, forced her breathing to remain even, held the smile on her face as though it had been carved. "I heard nothing. I can't help you at all."

.   .   .

"Bloody mud!" Martin shouted at the empty flat; nevertheless he felt a hero, felt proud of himself. He could see himself again as he had been the night before, running across mud and planking, crunching on brickdust, searching like the books prescribed for whoever it was that had attacked his woman . . . "Bloody mud!" he yelled, holding up his yellow-caked shoes, prancing towards the kitchen. "And it would have been—oh, yes, bloody indeed, if I'd . . ."

He threw open the door of the small boot cupboard, swinging his hand into a wide flourish. Then, without moving, stood.

"Mud," he said, in a voice suddenly low. "Bloody mud."

On the bottom shelf of the cupboard, half-hidden by a small tower built from empty tins of polish, lay a crumpled cloth. Its red-checked pattern was caked and obscured by smears of yellow, drying clay. Martin held up the shoes he carried. He stared at them, then at the cloth. With one fingernail he jabbed at the leather, dragged off a sliver of dried mud. Bending, he took another off the cloth. He let them lie side-by-side in his palm. He stared at them, his thoughts flinging jagged and haphazard about his brain, like dangerous shrapnel.

Suddenly he turned, ran along the passage, burst into Hassan's room. Innocently, its silence enveloped him. He hesitated, then opened the wardrobe. Hassan, he thought; Hassan, Hassan—flatmate, stranger: what did he know about him? Lies, it might be —for that muddy cloth had not been pressed into the shadows of the kitchen cabinet by anyone else. "Hassan, Hassan . . ." The name flew across his mind like a bombardment. Moving quietly, Martin began to search the room.

It was ten minutes later that he found what he was looking for. In the corner, flung behind a suitcase under the bed, a pair of Hassan's trousers. Martin stared at them; had Hassan been wearing them yesterday?

"Of course he was. Why else? . . ." he murmured.

Each leg was spattered almost to the knee with the same thick, yellow mud. He ran his hand across the dry clay's encrusting ridges.

"But what was he doing? What was he thinking of?" he asked himself, his voice a whisper. "Is he mad? Can he be a madman?"

But it was only mud, he thought. He had no idea where Hassan had been the day before; there would be an explanation. There was no reason why a man shouldn't get mud on his clothes: it was only mud, after all. Yet he knew, with a certainty he utterly refused to acknowledge, that this mud was the same he had wallowed through the night before, that it was evidence pointing to conclusions he would sooner or later have to face.

"It's nothing I could tell the police," Martin said, "but I'll watch him. Good God, yes, he'll have to be watched."

.　　　.　　　.

"Are you all right?"

Ricky smiled, but Martin looked down at her, frowning, concerned.

She said, "Trembly, when I think. But I try not to think."

"Nightmarish."

"Why? Why did he do it? What did he want?" Ricky had stopped smiling. Suddenly pale, she stared up at Martin, then turned away, laid her head against the deep back of her armchair, so that Martin could see her profile and the long, tensed muscles of her neck. "Who'd do it? Standing in the dark, waiting . . . But waiting for what? For me? Do you think for me, Martin? Because if it was . . . if it was for me, it was . . . it'd have to be—someone who knew me. Someone I knew. And that's a horrible thought. Looking at my friends, trying to guess, trying to make out if they could have . . ."

"It was no one like that," Martin said. (It was Hassan, he thought, certainly catching him unawares; it was Hassan, whom she knew and did not know) "It's ridiculous to think it was a friend. You know that none of the people we've met could behave like that, do a thing like that."

"Do I? I don't know anything about the people we've met. How do they behave to their lovers, for instance? What are their sexual quirks? How do they treat their children or their employees? What do they dream of, what do they think when they lie out somewhere, staring at the sky? We know damn-all about the people around us, Martin. It could have been anyone." She swung to face him again, her eyes dark and terrified. "Anyone at all."

Martin nodded, smiling a little now, the situation forcing him to a tenderness he had never before been able to express.

95

He said, "You mustn't care in that way, bother yourself with thoughts like that. It's not worth it—over some maniac, some poor, twisted bastard who can't help himself. You know there are people like that. They pick a place at random . . ."

"But it wasn't at random! He picked here because I live alone, because I'm a girl living on her own. Can't you see that?"

"He wouldn't have to be a friend of ours to know that. It doesn't take much to find out who's where in a block of flats like this."

Ricky looked at him for a moment, as if uncertain of what she should feel, then nodded. "Yes. That's true. So it's possible that it wasn't . . . But it's been horrible. I've been going over and over all the faces I've ever met, trying to fit . . . oh, hate or something—fury, madness—over them, trying to find traces of . . . Oh, I don't know . . ."

Quietly, she began to cry, and Martin bent down and sat on the arm of the chair beside her. Easily, he put his arms around her and pulled her head down to his lap and let her cry. She cried for a long time and then, quite suddenly, stopped crying and went to sleep. Holding her like that, hardly feeling the pain of his immobility, Martin let the hours fall on into the dusk. And as the time passed, he thought of Ricky and terror and the damage it would do; and thought of Hassan hiding in the darkness intent on murder, Hassan smiling and studious and quick over the housework, all the time intent on death, waiting for the moment when he would stand in shadow, tensed for ambush, Ricky his quarry.

"I wish I understood," he thought, but that was a lie; he no longer cared for reasons, explanations, the generalities of a liberal compassion. In a very precise way, perhaps because he was helpless, did not know how to act, he was discovering hatred.

. . .

"What did you say?"

It was the following morning. Martin, dressing-gowned and still slit-eyed from sleep, stood at his own door.

"Scotland Yard," the man on the doorstep repeated. He wore a dark, lightweight suit, a pale pink shirt, a tie discreetly flowered. His blond hair was crew-cut, his pink face shone with

96

the eagerness of a salesman.

"But what on earth? . . ." Martin began, then suddenly straightened. "It's not Ricky? That bastard hasn't had another go at? . . ."

"Perhaps if we talked inside, Mr. Prescott?"

"Yes. Of course . . ."

The policeman sat with a sigh into the cushions on Martin's couch. Martin himself, nervously to and fro, looked at him from time to time, short sideways glances of bewilderment and tension.

He said, "I'm sorry . . . your name—did you say . . ."

"Harroway. Detective-Sergeant."

"Ah. Yes. But, all the same, I don't . . ."

"I'm looking for a Mr. Burani."

"Hassan?"

"He lives here?"

"Certainly."

"Ah."

There was a pause. Almost irritably, Martin broke it.

"Well?"

"Mr. Burani's a friend of yours, sir?"

"No. Not exactly. He lives here. We share the flat. I advertised, and there he was."

"Yes. And he's been no bother?"

"Bother? I . . . I don't know . . ."

Mud, he thought; caked mud on a cloth, on trouser legs— meaningless. Yet now the police had come to him, hadn't he a duty? . . .

"Not bother," he muttered. "But . . ."

This time it was the policeman who politely broke the silence and Martin, as if for relief, blurted out his new suspicions of Hassan. Then, feeling ridiculous and at the same time guilty, he turned away.

"It's all nothing," he said. "Just a thought—there's lots of mud about, after all."

"A hell of a lot of mud, sir," Harroway genially agreed. "There's some been flung in Mr. Burani's direction—oh, not by you, sir," and he laughed, seeing Martin's suddenly indignant face swing towards him. "But I don't see why in the light of what you've said I shouldn't tell you my reasons for being here.

We received an anonymous telephone call implicating Mr. Burani in a murder."

"Murder!"

"Well?"

"Yes. I suppose—if he did attack Ricky . . . I mean, if it was Hassan I chased and if that was why he was running . . . But it's a word, isn't it—I mean, an enormous word, just to enter someone's life like this: 'murder.'"

Abruptly, he sat down. He could hardly face this confirmation of what he had suspected.

"Who was it?" he asked, his voice shaking a little. "Who was killed?"

"The manager of an off-licence."

"Off-licence?"

Meaninglessly, the words lay between them, hung like some pointless echo in the air. Martin pushed hair off his forehead. He asked, "Round here? Someone local?"

"No. But the woman who phoned was definite—named Mr. Burani, gave this address."

"Woman?"

"Yes."

"And here you are."

"Yes, sir."

"Well. What now?"

An hour later, among the glass partitions and the distant sounds of typewriter and telephone, Martin asked the question again, this time of a thin, sad-faced man who sat as if in private grief behind a bare desk and watched his every move with the wide, astonished eyes of a child.

"What now?"

The sad-faced man, Detective-Superintendent Melton, shifted on his official chair, made one or two indeterminate gestures. "Difficult," he said. "We're no further on. Can't base our case on the mud you found, can we?"

"No, I suppose you can't."

"Don't even know if there's a connection."

"No."

"We'd have to see if we can dig up Mr. Burani's associates. That'd be something, wouldn't it?"

"Associates?"

"Friends, sir."

"He had a girl-friend."

"You know her, sir?"

"No, I'm afraid I . . . Well, I met her once. At a party. He hadn't seen her for years and he came to this do with us and suddenly there was this woman . . . They'd know her, wouldn't they?"

"Who?"

"The people who gave the party!"

Detective-Superintendent Melton paused for a moment, then picked up his telephone. "Maybe you could find out for us, sir."

Martin nodded, took the receiver. As he dialled, he said, "But I haven't a great deal of time. There's a sort of prize giving I have to be present at . . ."

"When we have a line on Mr. Burani's girl-friend, sir, we . . ."

Martin spoke into the receiver. "Mr. Halling? Oh, Paul, it's Martin here—Martin Prescott. I wonder if you'd help me—I'm trying to trace a girl . . ."

. . . . .

". . . and for all these reasons the first prize goes to Durward and Jensen. In second place, with a design which in its meticulous concern for details and detailing is the more meritorious because he worked alone, the judges have placed the plans of Martin Prescott. In the third place are . . ."

"But that's marvellous!" Ricky cried, jumping high, arms and legs spread. "Marvellous!"

"And there was interest," Martin said, no longer in the portentous voice with which he had imitated authority. "The world stirred."

"It beat a path to your door?"

"Not quite—but it intimated that if I were prepared to beat a path to its door, I might very well find it open."

"Specifically?"

"Well, first within the company. A phone call from higher quarters, a sick smile from Harrison—and a place for me on the design consultancy committee."

"Which? . . ."

"I shall consider and then, I suspect, turn down."

"Because?"

"It's no more than a glorified liaison job; they hire architects to do the real work."

"There's a point to this conversation—expectation is at fever pitch . . ."

She stood in front of him, her fists clenched, her eyes wide, every muscle of her body witnessing to tension.

"Prepare the drum roll, attend the pooping of trumpets—Durward and Jensen have asked me to work with them."

"The winners?"

"None other."

"The deadly rivals?"

"The same."

"Why?"

"Because, they said, I too was on to something and they thought it was similar to what they were on to and why shouldn't we snuffle about after it together?"

"Why not indeed."

"I thought so."

"And money?"

"Oh, none of your assistant's pittance—it'd be the right journeyman class. On top of which there is . . ."

He hesitated and then they both shouted in unison, "The prize!"

Laughing, they embraced; then their tongues stopped sound. Mouth to mouth they rolled sideways on the black couch, their caresses, less than serious, hinting nevertheless at serious ecstasies to come. It was Ricky who, sprawled long-legged under his weight, turned her face away, rolled out from under his squirming.

"Coward," he said. His fingers trapped her leg, rose to curve about her right buttock; then travelled, probing under. Gasping, she weakened, leaning over him.

"No," she murmured, "Please. No."

With his cheek he began stroking the warmth of her groin and above him she closed her eyes, bent forward to accommodate him. Then pulled away a second time.

"Tell me—the holiday," she said, dry-voiced. She cleared her throat, went on, "What about the Peak and the holiday?"

"But all that's arranged," he yelled, and leaned back, laughing at the amazement on her face.

"Arranged!"

"I said to Harrison that I had to have a holiday. I had to consider the company's offer, I'd finished up the work he'd given he—I thought it was time I was off for a week or so."

"And he agreed?"

"He smiled. His lips parted as if they were a crack in some cheap china cup—I expect they're no more hygienic. His face went all mottled and I prayed for a stroke. But it was friendliness that was destroying him."

"So he agreed? He agreed there and then?"

"And I went out to buy a car for our holiday."

There was a pause after this. Ricky looked down at Martin, then walked away from him. Her face thus hidden, she said, "And Hassan?"

"Well?"

There was another pause. Then she shrugged. "I wasn't reasonable. It was the strain—the result coming, so much depending on it."

"You think he should come with us?"

"Why not? He helps—we'll need a handyman. And as long as he's got another girl with him . . ."

"Oh, that's understood. That's been explained."

"Why not spread the spoils of victory, then?"

"Near-victory."

"No. What isn't a defeat is victory."

"For people in our position, perhaps."

"Yes. For people in our position."

"So spread the fruits?"

"Why not? We've had Capability Brown—why not Cornucopia Prescott?"

Ricky laughed again, then shook her head as if hopeless and bent and kissed him.

.   .   .

Hassan stopped, walked into the road. He glanced into the windscreen of the parked van beside him. Among those who walked, reflected, down the evening pavement, the tall man in the olive-green sports coat sauntered as easily as any. Had been thus sauntering, along each street chosen more and more at random by Hassan, for the last two hours or more. Hassan crossed to the opposite pavement, lurked for a hesitant stride or two in front of a toy shop, watched the still-reflected tall men crossing a little higher up the street.

Thus tied together by the following man's attention, the two of them walked busy pavements, Hassan now and then twisting through the crowds in some store or queue or Underground station, only to find as he came out of an obscure exit into a back-street lost between great cliffs of white-tiled bricks that the tall man, a smile on his long, thin-jowled face, was still relaxed and watchful on his trail.

It was already dusk. Hassan jumped on a passing bus, climbed to the top deck, looked down to see in the stairway mirror the flash of olive-green, the face for a moment upturned, dark eyes looking deeply into his own; then the man had moved imperturbably inside. Hassan sat, looked down at the coagulate of car roofs, bit his lip. I'm found, he thought; they've asked, they've set the hounds on me, they've quartered the city and cut across my trail. They must know the other one is dead; who can this one be? Who have they sent, better than the last, quicker, deadlier: better, quicker, deadlier than me?

The bus rounded a church, rolled down a wide road. Then lights held it; a cinema rose on the right, its façade glittering with false promises. Hassan ran down the stairs, leaped to the pavement, crossed between the tails and jaws of the unending traffic. Behind him he heard a sudden scream of brakes; someone else had taken the direct path across that slow stream of metal. Not looking round, Hassan hurried into the cinema, bought a ticket for the circle, raced upstairs. He crossed the upstairs foyer, went through the doors on the other side, ran down three or four steps, then crouched, waited. After five minutes, no one had passed him. He ran down the stairs again, out into the darkening town. Hurrying down a wide pavement he turned his head; olive-green showed fifty yards away, long legs stretched to match his pace. He had achieved nothing.

Abruptly, he swung down a street that opened to his left. It was empty, sloped gently down the dusk. Behind him, he heard the soft shuffle of the man who followed. Closer, was he? Closing? Hassan wanted to turn, to stand and face the pursuer, to finish it once and for all. But training forced him on—"Find the battlefield of your choice; then fight on it," he remembered. But there was very little choice, very little time. The footsteps sounded nearer.

To his left, a tall, white gate, "FOR THE USE OF RESIDENTS ONLY". He turned, ran into shadow. Behind him the feet, swifter. He tried the latch of the gate, lifted it, pushed. The gate swung open, creaking slightly. Hassan pushed it to, ran down a short white-washed tunnel to come out in a wide asphalted space. All about rose the backs of tall apartment blocks. These over-shadowed the space; night had already settled here.

To Hassan's right there ran a narrow ash path and, as he turned down this, he heard the amplified groaning of the opened gate echoing down the tunnel behind him; then silence. He crouched, looking about him. He had seconds. Beside him was a low wall, beyond it bushes, a narrow lawn, then the dark windows of a ground-floor flat. Hassan vaulted brickwork, then lay flat. Pressed against the earth, he could hear the swift rhythms of his heartbeat, the fluttering sound of his own terror.

A foot slid on ash, scraping. Then the easy footfalls of a practised hunter; these closing, softly close. Hesitating. Not looking up, his muscles tense, Hassan knew the other was beyond the wall, not two feet away, held at bay by darkness and the few courses of crumbling brick. But Hassan did not move. Let him search, he thought, let him worry at the night for a while, let him whirl and snatch at sudden sounds—then I'll be the stalker. Lying face down in dead leaves, he almost smiled; not breathing, tensed for silence, immobile as the ground itself.

The other moved off, hunting; Hassan could hear those trained, soft-treading feet step off the path and turn towards the far side of the apshalt square.

At the dog's sudden bark, he almost screamed; then rolled to face the pointed muzzle of a dachshund which, legs braced and shoulders hunched, poured out its stream of invective and suspicion.

"Leave it!" he whispered. "Good dog!"

But the dachshund shouted on; and on the far side of the wall Hassan could hear the returning footsteps of the man who had been sent to find and kill him. He crouched, his legs braced, his fingers tensed for violence. Behind him, the dog danced and barked.

"You!"

That was another voice, cutting raucously through noise and silence. Hassan stopped breathing; the dog too whined, then became quiet.

"You there!"

A man ran heavily across the asphalt. Lights came on; here and there a window was opened. The dachshund ran past Hassan and out into the open space beyond the wall.

"Me?" The voice was quiet, composed; and very close.

Hassan fell flat, grovelled in shadow.

"Yes, you. What are you doing here?"

"I have moved here—close to here. My cat is lost as a result of the move."

"All right. If I see it I'll let you have it."

"You?"

"I'm the porter here. What's the cat like?"

"Black. One white foreleg—the left. Its name is Emir."

"All right. I'll look out for it."

"I cannot go on searching for it myself?"

"No. I don't know you. I don't know if your story's true. If I let you go on and you're a burglar or some bloody Peeping Tom, I'd look pretty stupid, wouldn't I?"

"Yes, I can see that."

"All right then."

Two pairs of feet moved away, followed by the now desultory yapping of the dachshund. In a moment, this sounded in sad, hollow sequence from the tunnel that led to the white gate. Windows closed, curtains were twitched into place. Hassan got slowly to his feet, brushed wet leaves off his jacket.

"And don't hang about there!" he heard the porter shout, his tone one of aggressive warning. Hassan vaulted the wall, ran across the open space, turned right along the path he found there. To his left, an opening between buildings, a metal gate at the end of it. Hassan ran down this, tried the gate; it was locked. He stretched, pulled, levered with his toes, lifted himself to the gate's broad top, then jumped into the alleyway beyond. Quietly he walked to the end of this, then knelt and peered up and down the road it led to. The pavements were empty. Between the pools of lamplight night gathered, but in these darknesses, nothing moved. Hassan waited five minutes, ten minutes, fifteen. Finally, satisfied he was alone, he got to his feet, walked thoughtfully back to the main and noisy streets he had left, hailed a prowling taxi, settled with his eyes closed in the back.

.　　　.　　　.

"I don't think I can stay in London."

"Really?"

Laura stood by the window, her hand clutching the drawn curtain. What should she say, she wondered. How speak calmly, how dissemble fear?

"I think I must go," Hassan said in a lower voice. "I think I have to."

"Have to?"

He stared at Laura's back, at the stiffened lines of her body. Her voice was as cold and withdrawn, as harsh as when they had met once more at that party.

"What is the matter?" he asked.

She whirled, to stare at him with such a look of glittering fury that he took a short step backwards.

"The matter?" she echoed, an edge of hysteria in her voice now.

"You are very cold, very angry. I cannot understand . . ."

"It's a mood," she said, curtly, turning away again.

"Martin has arranged it," Hassan said, hesitantly. "You said you might . . . that if he asked us to go with him to Derbyshire, you might be able to manage it."

"That's finished. I can't come."

"I need you there. With me."

"Need me for what?"

"For . . . protection. To hold me, to keep me ordinary."

"Ordinary? You? When you know what you are!"

"I am . . ." But he hesitated, not knowing any longer how to describe himself.

Laura said, "I can't come, anyway. With short notice like this . . ."

"You won't come?"

105

"I won't."

"Not for me, to help me?"

"No!" Laura whirled on this word, her mouth wide with hatred. The sound of her words was ragged, very high, harsh. "No! I've helped you—that's the one time. And the last, the only . . . Now that's finished. I've thought about that, about you, about this room, trying to see you, to see myself; to make sense of what we are, what sort of couple we are . . . But all that's rubbish. It's dead, beyond ghosts—we're no couple because you've gone. You're not there any more."

"I am here." He stretched his hand out, but she shrank away.

"No. That's meaningless: the flesh, the skin and warmth— that's all lies. And I've stopped believing those lies, they don't deceive me any more . . ."

"I love you. That is truth. I suffered when I thought I would never see you again. When we met, I was happy. I have been happy since."

"Happy!" She stared at him once more, her eyes wide with the fascination of horror. "But do you think I don't know?"

There was a long pause after this. Hassan, frowning, tried to understand her mind, her discoveries and intentions. How had she learned of Ricky, he wondered; of what he felt for Ricky. What had been found out?

"Last night," she shouted. "Just last night! Do you imagine I don't know. Do you think I'm mad or blind or so stupid that . . ."

"But she didn't . . ." Hassan blankly began, but Laura cut him off.

"The whiskey! The off-licence!"

Hassan felt his face stiffen as though it had been set in plaster of Paris. "The off-licence," he repeated, giving away nothing.

"You were the last there. You said he was shut. He was found dead, killed; scientifically, they said, scientifically murdered."

"They?"

"The police."

"So you said that I was the last who . . ."

"I didn't say anything. I had no time, no courage. Not even the will."

"He must have gone back to the shop. There was no one there when I . . . It was shut. I knocked on the door. There was no one there."

"Scientifically beaten, scientifically killed. You were there. You said he'd gone, but he was there. God knows what you did, what he said and you did; or why. But he was there and for some reason . . . If he'd come back he wouldn't have opened the door. He lived there; he had a flat over the shop. For God's sake! With its own front door for visitors—do you think all his visitors would have trampled through his shop too . . . You said he was shut but he was open, he was there; he must have said something, done something . . . Or perhaps not even that, perhaps you haven't even that excuse; no reasons at all. Just someone in front of you and . . . Like that last time! Easy, I suppose—like the last time."

Trembling, Hassan stood silently. He looked at the floor in front of him like a reprimanded schoolboy. He felt nothing. He heard her voice and wished it would stop. He thought he would have a headache later on.

"And then you come here, you talk about happiness, holidays; some sort of future, a continuing present . . . You must be insane! You must really be insane!"

In a low voice Hassan said, "That is why I need you. To keep me from myself. To hold me to sanity and to stop me from . . . I need you to protect me."

"All that's too late."

"Too late." He did not hear these words, although he repeated them. He seemed self-contained, held by what he was as though by walls. "Too late, too late."

"Yes. Much, much too late." Her voice hated him. "I should have known, I should have realised that—what?—that you'd been changed? Or that you'd always been like that, always a killer, but had kept it hidden? Or that you hadn't even kept it hidden but I'd simply not seen it? But I should have realised—when you first spoke to me, or that night at the party . . . At any rate after we'd . . . after you'd come to me and told me about that man, about the first one you . . . If it was the first one? If it was the first? But then, in any case; I should have known. I shouldn't have helped you, I should never have seen you again. Instead . . ."

"You won't come with me?" He asked this flatly, without emotion.

"It's finished. Can't you realise it? There's nothing to be done or said between us, no more 'together'. Can't you see that you've destroyed—yes, murdered!—murdered that too?"

"You won't? You'd refuse that? But it's arranged—Martin said . . . In any case, I have to leave. They've found me again."

"Those people? Like the one you . . . the first one?"

"Yes. I suppose when he did not go back . . ."

He glanced at her, then looked elsewhere; seeing nothing. She bit her lip, but after a while shrugged, set obstinacy on her face. In a chill silence they faced each other, but like strangers momentarily forced to share a room.

"They will kill me," he said, at length. His voice was still steady, still flat. "If I stay in London they will find me and kill me."

"It's your situation, your war," she insisted shrilly. "I had nothing to do with it. You can't make me responsible. Not in any way."

"But I have to go away. I might never come back. Even if it is only a holiday, I would like you there, I would like you with me."

But this was a lie, he thought; he did not want her with him, or near him, or in his life. Ricky stirred in his mind like a foetus in a pregnant belly.

"Will you come with me?" he asked, this time with a touch of desperation in his tones.

"No. How many times? . . . No. I won't. It's over. There's nothing to be said. Don't you understand that you're a . . . a monster, that I can't see you, can't be in the same room with you, the same house, without horror and shame? Shame!"

She thought of the heat his caresses had carried, of herself flung to and fro by them, white on white, reigned by the sensations he stroked out of her depths. She thought she might vomit; and indeed turned her head suddenly to one side in precaution.

Thus shuddering, she was not ready for his sudden movement towards her. She would have stepped back if he had not taken her gently by the upper arm, his fingers softly across the skin.

"You cannot have changed," he said, but without warmth, as if he did not mean it, or did not care.

"I? I can't have? And you?"

"You love me," he asserted, in the same dead voice.

Abruptly, she was afraid. She looked up at him, her head craning round towards him. She licked dry lips, frowned as if trying to concentrate.

"But think of it," she said. "Of what you've done, of what you've . . ."

He smiled, interrupting her. "Whatever they have turned me into, you might change me back."

"If you had help," she muttered, shaking her head. "A doctor . . ."

"What will I tell him?"

He smiled again, the expression bitter, his eyes cold.

Laura shook her head. "It's not possible. I can't. I loved you . . . thought I loved you. But . . ."

"Thought!"

"Well, loved you. I don't know. But now . . . No. I can't. There's no way."

"I need you."

"No."

"I need you to come."

"No, I can't."

"Please."

The fingers on the arm bit deeper. She tried to squirm away, then stood still. She noticed there was a slime of sweat on his forehead. The house was very quiet.

"What good would it do?" she asked, her voice cracking.

"I have said I need you."

"I can't," she said again. "I can't."

Very formally he said, "I want you to come with me."

"No," she whispered. "I won't."

He broke her neck. The blow was single; the fingers of his left hand let go their hold of her arm, he stepped back, the blade of his right hand whipped from left to right: he felt the snap of bone. She fell forward and to her left. Blood coiled a short way, slowly, from her right nostril.

Hassan stood, trembling, alone in the silent house, the empty world.

"I asked you," he said. "Please come with me."

Laura lay face down, her right shoulder higher than her left. She had entered the indifference of the dead, was receding from him, from his needs and demands; had thus escaped, never to learn how he had punished her.

He sat down, moving very carefully, as if at any moment he might by carelessness break something. He did not lean back but upright, his eyes wide open, stared ahead of him. Now and then a slow shudder moved his shoulders and his head. Otherwise he did not move. In the hall outside, the clock chimed off an hour, then its half-hour, then the next full hour: eleven o'clock.

"Well, then," Hassan muttered. He sighed unsteadily, looked slowly round the room. He nodded to himself as if pleased to discover everything in its usual place.

"Well, then," he said again.

He sank back in the chair and closed his eyes; perhaps he slept. It was one in the morning before he moved again. He opened his eyes and with a quick movement stood up, walked quickly to the lavatory; there he defecated, washed his hands with a soap of which he recognised the scent, then very carefully adjusted his maroon tie in front of the mirror. With his hands thus at his own throat, he stopped moving. For almost twenty minutes he stood like this, his face expressionless and his dark eyes staring past its pale reflection. Then he went on settling his tie, his movements easy, his manner relaxed; it was as if he had not noticed that time had passed.

As he walked into the living room, now so abruptly misnamed, he seemed brisk, new-washed, almost as if about to whistle. But the high-shouldered body, its face hidden, stopped him. For a moment he checked his stride, biting his lip in bewilderment. Stopping beside the body, he hovered, his manner expectant, as if he half-thought Laura would at any moment get to her feet and in an unconcerned, matter-of-fact voice make some easy, everyday request. But Laura had no more movement in her.

Hassan walked slowly backwards, sat down in a deep arm-chair. He could see the hump of Laura's buttocks under the skirt, then the long slopes of her thighs, the bright calves, finally the feet, the tips of the shoes closer together than the heels.

"Perhaps I am mad," he whispered. He nodded slowly, thoughtfully biting his lower lip. "Yes, perhaps."

He felt suddenly relieved, having faced this idea of himself. He shrugged, leaned well back in the chair. He knew he was not mad. He had, after all, given Laura every chance, had begged her, had said "Please".

"She knew me," he murmured. "She knew what to expect of me."

If she had not argued, if she had not disagreed . . . He was no different from before. He stretched out his right hand, felt the skin, the warmth, the hidden network of bone. He was just the same, after all. He had changed in only one particular.

"Death's so easy," he said.

He had learned that, and so had changed. Death was easy, the bringing of death simple and logical. He considered this, then slowly smiled. He felt calm, relaxed; earlier, he had been worried and now he wondered why.

In the hall, the clock struck twice. Hassan sighed, got to his feet again, ran upstairs. To the left of the landing was a narrow door. Hassan opened this, dragged a deep, brown trunk, hooped with metal, out of the cupboard's darkness. He put this on his shoulder, ran downstairs once more. Working, he felt absorbed, concentrated; almost happy.

Laura was inert, but light. For a moment the way she hung against his hands worried him; then he had turned her over, flipped her casually into the trunk. Her skirt slid a long way up her dead, white thigh and Hassan carefully covered all that skin and shut the lid of the trunk.

The Triumph Herald rolled with hardly a sound down the shallow slope that led into the road, then on a little way between the stunted suburban trees, before Hassan started the engine and began his drive across London.

He lost his way once, but realised it almost immediately. It took him not more than eight minutes to find the proper route again. It pleased him to be so accurate; he had only travelled along it once, but his year's forced training as assassin had not been in vain and now he remembered the bends and hedges, the fences and hill-tops and sudden turnings as if by instinct.

When he stopped the car it was in the raw grey of dawn's beginning. As he shut the door, a blackbird began to sing somewhere to his right. A cold breeze snatched fitfully at leaves and green-brown grass.

Hassan picked the trunk out of the car's boot, set it across his shoulders and, breathing easily, carried it swiftly through the gate

III

to his left and up the small rise beyond.

The water of the gravel pit looked black. The breeze moved over it, roughening it, piling it up in small pimples of water that seemed very cold. Hassan halted on the top of the ridge, looked left and right, then ran down towards the clump of bushes. There was a sudden shout of leaves and branches as he flung the trunk to the ground, an explosion of snapping twigs as if he had lit a fire. He stood still, waited for challenge or curiosity —early hunter or late poacher. But no one called. Only the birds built up, species by species, their welcome to the light.

When he tilted the trunk, the body that had been Laura's tumbled sideways from it, to lie stiffly among the sparse grass and rotting leaves. Its face glared up, one eye stiffly wide, the other nearly closed. The sky it seemed to watch for portents remained blank, lightening through a million greys towards the blue of daylight.

Hassan dropped four or five dark stones between the body's cooling breasts. When he lifted it, these dropped, to be held in bulges by the thin belt around the waist.

At the edge of the clump of bushes, Hassan stopped, the body across his shoulders, the single staring eye now regarding the ground. When he was sure that the morning still held no watchers, he ran forward the seven paces that were between him and the water. Without hesitation he swung round, using his momentum to throw the body from him, watching as splay-legged it flew, diving across death, to splash into the pond's darkness.

In the water, it seemed to hesitate. Then the stones about its middle forced it down, so that for a moment it was as if standing on some submerged rock two or three feet below the surface. The open eye momentarily reflected the grey dawn light.

Hassan made a movement with his right hand, trying from this distance to force the body out of sight. As if in response, it began to droop, to slide towards oblivion, tilting backwards as it sank. The soft skirt dragged sideways, then up. Hassan could see the fading tan of stockings, the white skin of the parted thighs, then pale green pants. The dark pubic hair curled in a vivid triangle beneath these, and as the body tilted again, to lie for a moment on its back just below the troubled surface, Hassan felt a sudden sexual excitement. Unconsciously he smiled, put

PART FOUR

Many a green isle needs must be
In the deep wide sea of Misery.
                              Shelley.

"But will you?" Martin shouted. "Will you be there? I've done it now, it's arranged—and will you be there?"

"Did you know his Laura's disappeared?"

Martin stared at Detective-Superintendent Melton, then turned sharply away, as if at an order. On the desk a telephone rang, then was abruptly silenced.

"Yes," Melton said. "She's gone. Left a note for her husband. Very methodical. Typewritten."

"Bit unemotional," Martin murmured, but looked down at the floor.

"Yes. We thought that. We'll have a good glance at the signature."

"The signature?"

"See if it's hers."

"She might have meant it. She's supposed to be coming with us."

"I know. That's why I asked you to call. You haven't seen her?"

"It's tomorrow we're off. I wouldn't have, would I?"

"Well, you haven't, so . . ."

Martin stood again, marched to his left, then hesitated, turned, sat down again.

"You'd better be there," he said, still savage. "You and your boys . . . Up there, in that country . . . it's rough, up there; mountains, cliffs—it's not called the Peak District for nothing."

"It's lonely, isn't it?" Melton said.

"That's the point, for God's sake!"

"Where it's lonely, we can watch everything. Everyone. It's the cities that are too much for us—too many people, too many anonymous demands and desires, too many shoulders rubbing. Out in the open, you can see a stranger for miles."

"Yes. Yes. You must be right. But it's lives at stake—mine, Ricky's . . ."

"You haven't told her?"

"That she's bait?"

"It's your choice. You could tell her—or we could put a policewoman in as a double when it got tough or something . . ."

"No. I haven't told her yet. I don't know what to say. It's not even that she wouldn't go through with it—she'd do it. But she'd be terrified, it'd be a nightmare . . . And what if it was all for nothing? If we were wrong or you arrested him in any case or . . . She'd never trust me again. Would she? No. It's either to be done like this or not done at all."

There was a pause after this. Melton did not move, but peered, sad-faced, at the grain of his desk's wood. Martin fidgeted, swinging his head from side to side as if to avoid some weight. He lit a cigarette, sucked at it irritably.

He said, "It's got to be done. For her protection too. If she's a victim, a potential victim . . . It's for her sake too."

Melton suddenly straightened in his seat. "Now you've realised it. She's in danger now, whether Burani comes with you or ostensibly stays behind. It's not my place to put ideas in your head or to influence your decision—but if he's what we think he is, she's marked for violence, this girl-friend of yours. She really is."

Martin nodded, spat smoke at the ceiling. "Yes. I know."

"So, since the situation exists, let's try and control it. Minimise the danger. Have police protection . . ."

"But it's not that, is it? You want him to make a move. If he knew that you coppers were sitting on every hilltop he'd never touch her—but he isn't going to know that, is he? And you want him to touch her. Well, isn't that true?"

"Yes," Melton said, quite simply. His face, under its normal melancholy, was expressionless. "But we can't protect her for ever, Mr. Prescott. The man must be caught now, or he'll try another time. If he's what we think he is."

"And we do, don't we?"

"We have three reasons. None of them's enough alone, but the three together . . . There's the attack on your fiancée. There's the fact that his Laura lived a hundred yards from that off-licence. And there's the fact that a woman spoke to us . . . and a woman's missing."

"Laura?"

"Yes."

"With a note?"

"Typewritten."

"Yes."

Martin bit his lower lip, then sighed. "But you'll watch? You'll keep a real watch?"

"The best men. Do you imagine we can afford to take chances?"

"If Ricky dies . . ."

Melton said, hastily, "Not that this is an official plan."

"No?"

"Under no circumstances. We'd never hear the end of it."

"So, if everything goes all right, your boys . . ."

"Acting on information received . . ."

"Ride up in the nick of time . . ."

"Warrant in pocket . . ."

"Like the U.S. Fifth in the last reel."

Melton nodded ponderously, his eyes brightly on Martin's face.

"I think our policemen are marvellous," Martin said bitterly.

Melton shrugged. "A society gets the police it deserves. Like everything else it has. If the hallmark of ours is hypocrisy, that's the kind of coppers you'll have. We have to work within the system. We were invented for that."

"First the Singing Postman, now the Thinking Copper."

Melton shrugged again. "Are we in business, Mr. Prescott?"

Martin stood up. "Jesus, what choice do I have? It's no fun living with a potential murderer. Yes, it's on."

"The itinerary holds?"

"Yes. I've written it all out."

Melton nodded. "We'll have observers on the road. Nothing conspicuous—the occasional car, or a man in the hedge. Just to see you progress as planned."

"He won't make a move until we're there."

"He's a nutter, Mr. Prescott. A madman. He might move any time the whim comes over him."

"Who's to hold him then, Superintendent? Who's to fill the gap till your boys come?"

"We'll be within minutes of you for the whole journey. But as to those minutes—four, say, or five—I'm afraid they'll be up to you, sir. Unless you can think of some way of adding a constable to your party. I know it's hard, it exceeds my authority, it's probably immoral—but what alternative do I have?"

And Melton smiled with a grim melancholy across the desk at Martin.

.   .   .

Martin said, "Listen, I've sunk my winnings in a jolly pleasant little banger and I'm dying to use it. The open road, freedom, hair blowing free like all those people in the petrol ads . . . Instead, here we are . . ."

"I know," Hassan cut in. "I know that."

Ricky put a hand on Martin's sleeve. "You can see he's worried," she murmured.

And, can I? Martin thought. Is it just Laura's lateness that's bothering Hassan? The late Laura . . . is that a macabre joke?

He felt himself staring across the table at Hassan, so blinked, looked away. For a moment he seemed to be giddy, the world swung about him, he might have been at sea.

"You told her here?" he asked. "In this place?"

"It is a café we have used," Hassan said. He glanced around, then stood. "I will try and telephone her." Turning away, brushing between the bent backs of the coffee-drinkers, the gateau-eaters, he made his way towards the narrow telephone box in the corner.

Through the glass door he could see Martin and Ricky looking anxiously about them. Once Martin glanced at his watch, shrugged his irritation. Hassan dialled, keeping one finger on the telephone's bridge; he spoke into the dialling tone.

He said, "I can see you, Ricky. But you have not seen me. You think I have my place in a kitchen; you have no idea of power." His voice was soft, very even. He smiled a little. "Of my power. No idea."

Until this moment, he had not thought of himself as powerful, had hardly considered himself at all. Now, thinking of death, remembering his hands in controlled motion—controlled by what, he wondered; then stifled this thought—remembering the long bodies so suddenly inert, so utterly modified, he understood for the first time his strength.

"If I touched your hair," he whispered to the unanswering

telephone, "would you know what my hands have done? If I caressed you, would you feel that? Would you cringe, would you move away, would you understand? If you were naked, if you realised my force, if my two hands pressed you apart, if you were opened, would you know then? Will you discover, will you understand—that death is easy, after all, that I know what the limits are, that I have believed lies all my life? Death is easy, Ricky; the meantime is difficult—you could make it simpler. Will you realise that I have had a revelation and will you therefore end the struggling, the denials? There is an insistence in the moment, in strength, in the frontiers of life where I live now. Can you understand? . . ."

He spoke in a daze, his eyes half-closed. He only partly understood what he said, only distantly heard it. He felt comfortable, happy, warmly relaxed.

Martin, hammering abruptly on the door, dragged him from dreams. Hassan nodded, said, "Goodbye," put the receiver down. He licked his lips, all the time, the full lips dark-red under the black moustache, and stepped out of the telephone box.

"Well?"

Hassan shrugged. "Goodbye."

"What?"

"She can't come. Her husband has had an accident. They are bringing him to London at the moment."

"Accident?"

"You know he is an engineer. Something fell on him. I do not know what it was. She was very upset."

Joining them, "Why upset?" Ricky asked, and Martin passed on these lies.

"So, goodbye," Hassan said. He smiled, a little woodenly; a man bravely setting aside disappointment.

Martin and Ricky looked at each other.

"I don't know," Ricky said in a low voice. "I don't know."

"For my part, it's fine. But if you don't want to have a threesome . . ."

"No," Hassan put in. "I know how you feel. Having a third always with you . . ."

"Nonsense." Martin clapped his on the shoulder. "In any case, if you can see the difficulty . . ."

Ricky said, "Look, we'd be too busy to bother with you very

much. Too busy with each other. We don't often have time together. But the house is big enough, the cases are packed . . .
so if you think you can stand a week or so largely on your
own . . ."

Hassan nodded. "I have brought work," he said. He held up
a small case. Inside, his hidden weapons lay strapped into their
places. Hassan smiled and Martin, who knew about work, smiled
back.

"We'd be glad to have someone share some of the chores," he
pointed out.

"Well, as a sort of distant partner, if you really want me to
come," Hassan said, "I would be delighted."

They climbed into the faded Zodiac Martin had bought the
day before, Hassan silent, the other two giggling like children
at term's end.

"Everybody ready?" Martin asked.

"Yes," Ricky shouted, and "Oh, yes," Hassan quietly agreed.

"Right, then. *En avant!*"

With a scrabbling of tyres he whirled the car from the kerb
and into the traffic, its bonnet, by the accidents of topography,
already pointing north. Fifty yards away, in a shop doorway, a
tall, dark-skinned man briefly rubbed his narrow, black moustache, then took a notebook from his pocket, wrote for a moment.
Not bothering to put it back, he ran towards a white Jaguar
parked beside the pavement. The pages riffled against his hand
as he swung open the door, climbed in.

· · ·

"They're off the M1, sir," Harroway said.

Melton nodded. "The others are up there?"

"Yes, sir. It's good, broken country. They're dressed as
hikers and shepherds and what-not—it ought to be all right."

"It's going to have to be all right, Harroway. A hell of a risk
is being taken—and not by us. And if it goes wrong . . ."

"I know, sir. The dole."

"Right. No pension, no rank, no job."

Harroway sighed. "All the same, sir, Prescott was right. If
this Burani's got his sights set on that girl, he's going to have
to be stopped. Otherwise . . ."

"If the Aliens Department were a bit quicker . . ."

"Illegal entry, sir? It's not what we want."

"No. But it'd be safer."

"We can always stop him when we know for certain. If it's to be deportation, that is."

"I know. But when it's a murderer . . . In any case, he might have permission. He was a student. There's a special dispensation for them."

"If he was a student, sir."

"Bolling's checking on that. But I'll bet he was. I bet he was registered and certificated and *bona fide*. So he's going to have to do something to blot his copybook before we can move."

"Like murder, sir?"

"For instance. Yes. Murder."

Morosely, the Detective-Superintendent ran his pencil across the desk, watching it as if he were an augur on the look-out for portents.

.   .   .

The white Jaguar hooted once, then eased out to pass them. Martin hardly glanced at it, but held steadily to his own course and speed. The white car moved forward, then, slowing, seemed to hang.

"It's not going by," Ricky said, in indolent surprise.

As though tied to their car, the Jaguar moved beside them; then closed. Hassan frowned, leaned towards his window, peered across at the other car. Suddenly, he stiffened.

"No!" he exclaimed. "No!" He turned to Martin. "You must hurry!"

"Friends?" Martin asked.

Ricky shifted nervously, turning to look at the car still floating as if noiseless beside them.

Hassan said, "No. Not friends."

"There's a van behind us." Martin glanced at the mirror, then at the road in front. He pressed on the accelerator and the three of them leaned back against the surge. But the Jaguar stayed where it was, and the van behind them closed.

"The verge!" Hassan shouted. "On there, then brake . . ."

Martin nodded, watched the low, grassy bank flying past on the left.

123

"But who are they?" Ricky asked, breathlessly. "Who are they, Hassan?"

Hassan did not turn round. His right hand hung inside his jacket. His black eyes stared at the car beside them. Inside, two men, dark, long-faced, the driver with a thin moustache, drove as if they were alone on the road. Behind them, the blue van loomed; it seemed to shut them in, to be harrying them like a sheepdog.

"They're nearer," Ricky called, pointing. The Jaguar was edging in. To the right, the bank fell back from the road, a worn verge broadened. Martin swung the car sharply, the wheels hammered on uneven turf. At the same moment, the Jaguar cut in; behind them the van swung right, then left. There was the sigh of kissing metal, a tearing sound, the light carillon of breaking glass. Ricky screamed, falling sideways. The front of the van cut off their right-hand doors; in front of them, the ditched Jaguar held them like a barricade.

Doors slammed. Three man ran, one carrying a pistol. Inside Martin's car, something crashed, then crashed again. For no reason, he thought, one of the advancing men staggered sideways, then fell on his face.

"What is it? What is it?" Ricky asked in a high, strained voice.

"Keep down!" Hassan shouted. He opened his door, threw himself sideways. Martin, glancing, could see him roll, come to a crouch. The windscreen smashed and scattered. He ducked, then threw himself out of the near-side door. Beside him, a small explosion sounded; he knew what it was now—Hassan's unexpected pistol, miraculously produced. Another of the attackers fell, shouting.

A thin man, moving easily, came round the back of Martin's car, a knife brightly in his hand. Not thinking at all, Martin threw himself forward, his head like a ram's butting deep into the attacker's belly. He could hear the man retch, felt him fall away. From his outflung right hand, the knife flew in a sunlit parabola, to fizzle out like a rocket behind the dark-green hedge.

Martin lay, panting, fear catching up with him. A bullet howled off stone, cutting twigs and leaves as it curved on its unpredictable path. Someone shouted, an engine suddenly roared.

For a moment, Martin's heart moved: that was the answer! They would be free, rid of Hassan, rid of threat and danger. But he turned away, his head down; a Hassan at liberty might remain intent on harm to Ricky. And if he did, how would she be safe unless Martin at least knew where he was? No, he and Hassan were indissolubly together, tied by a marriage of convenience from which perhaps only death would part them.

Hassan said, "I do need you. First, because you are in danger; if they find you and realise you cannot answer their questions about me, they will kill you. You have to realise that that is the sort of people they are. In the second place, we must travel a long way and I need someone with whom to share the driving. And on the island, there are two cottages—they should be occupied."

"It's an adventure," Martin said, his face stiff with cameraderie. He nodded at Hassan. "We have to help the flat-mate, anyway. That's only good manners."

He climbed down from the van, helped Ricky load it up with their luggage. Hassan stood to one side, the pistol still loosely in his hand, not watching them. On the road, two or three cars swept by, faces pink at the window, then whirled away, their curiosity without answers.

What if Melton did not find them, Martin wondered. What if he were to be left alone to cope with Hassan? What if Hassan's friends were to catch up with them again?

"What if we get arrested for driving a stolen van?" Ricky asked, and Martin started, hearing her voice echo the phrase in his thoughts.

"Stolen?"

"I bet it is."

"We will change it," Hassan said. "Quite soon. Part exchange."

"What with? And if we can't prove we own it . . ."

"I have money. Everything will be arranged. Now, are we ready?"

He waved a little vaguely with his right hand, noticed that it still held the gun, put this away under his armpit. Then he climbed up beside Martin and Ricky. Martin started the engine, reversed, then turned. Side-by-side like loving friends, they bumped into the road.

It was ninety seconds later that the grey Cortina, passing, suddenly put its bonnet down, like the head of a bucking horse, and stopped in a scattering of gravel. Doors swung, two men in brown sports coats ran, then stood in perplexity beside Martin's abandoned car. The police cover had arrived, seven minutes too late for the action.

.   .   .

"Abandoned?" Melton said.

Sergeant Harroway nodded. "The Zodiac. Yes, sir. And smashed. Then blood on grass. And witnesses who saw a blue van drive off."

"The one we found in Sheffield?"

"I think so, sir."

"But all three of them showed up there."

"Yes, sir."

Melton stood up, walked restlessly up and down once, then sat down.

"It's bloody odd," he said.

"I know it is," Harroway agreed. "Who were they fighting?"

"And we'd set the whole thing up . . ."

"Maybe this Prescott's bent in some way."

Melton shook his head. "No. One can't ever be sure, but I don't think so. He was worried about that girl of his—that was honest, I'm certain."

"He hasn't got a message to us."

"No. He hasn't. But it wouldn't be easy—she doesn't know Burani's dangerous, and Burani doesn't know Prescott knows."

"Yes, sir. That is pretty ticklish."

"Yes."

There was another pause. Then Melton said, "All right. Alert everyone about the Vauxhall they bought in Sheffield. Especially the north—they seem to be heading in that direction. Watch the ferries to Ireland, and Glasgow Docks, and the airports there. And I suppose we need an eye on the East Coast ports— Newcastle, Aberdeen and so on. Means liaison with the Scots and I hope they don't feel these days we ought to put it through Interpol."

Harroway laughed, but briefly.

"All the same," Melton went on in a low voice. "I hope we find them soon. I'm certain that Burani's bent. There's no record for him at all—but there's no sign of that woman of his. She didn't leave with them, her husband doesn't know where she is and then the note . . ."

"The signature?"

"Yes, you were out, weren't you, Harroway? It's not hers. So perhaps you'd put a call out about her, too. We've got a photograph . . . But I wish I knew where my bait had got to."

Moodily, he tapped with his pencil on the desk. Harroway, who knew the mood, went quietly out of the office.

. . . . .

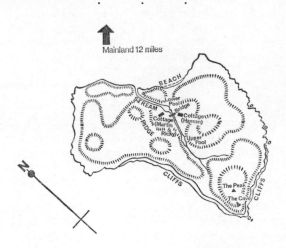

LACHAN
Scale: half inch = one mile

Lachan, Hassan's island, his last hiding-place, sat lop-sided in the sea before them. To the right it wore a thin frill of foam, to the left, pink and grey cliffs lifted in a low line out of the Irish Sea. The island seemed to rise, swing, then sink, as their boat rolled over the slow waves.

"Nearly there," the fisherman who was ferrying them yelled over the stammer of the outboard.

"Looks bleak," Martin said. He sat, leaning forward, beside the fisherman, who was called Duncan McLeod; his left arm was round Ricky. Opposite them Hassan, his expression morose, looked over his shoulder at the approaching island.

"Aye, well," said Duncan McLeod, "a few people might take the bleakness from it."

"Or it might put a touch of bleakness on the people," Martin suggested.

"Two cottages," Duncan McLeod pointed out. "Water, fish in the sea, shell-fish on the rocks, rabbits in the heather, birds and the eggs of birds . . . A fine place if you can hunt at all."

"Are any of us hunters?" Ricky asked.

"No," Martin replied, laughing. "Look at Hassan—what kind of pose is that for a man of action?"

Hassan smiled a thin smile, his yellowing face folding to accommodate this grimace. He looked as if snarling, but said in the manner of one good-humoured, "It is certain that whatever action I might contemplate, it will not be sea-fishing."

"Oh yes, these small boats," Duncan McLeod murmured. He shook his head in commiseration. "If you're not used to these small boats . . ."

It was twenty minutes later that the boat's bottom grated on shingle. Duncan McLeod, high-booted, was over the side, heaving the boat to stillness, then helping them carry the luggage they had brought and the packages they had purchased. They helped to push him off, then stood in a line, their feet in the cool water, as he let the screw of the outboard into the water.

"I'll be back, then, in a week," Duncan McLeod called.

"In a week," Martin confirmed, and Duncan McLeod nodded and tugged the engine's starter before waving once and settling to his steering.

Ricky waved back, then all three of them stood silently watching the boat rise and buck and, slowly, diminish, until it began to dissolve in the salt haze that half-hid the mainland hills twelve miles away.

"We'd better get settled," Martin warned. "It's nearly four now."

"The cottages are through there," Hassan told them. He pointed to an uncertain path that ran up from the narrow strip of shingle, across wind-cropped turf, to disappear over the low hump that here lined the coast-line. "I found them once, on holiday. They belonged to an old lady—her family used to live here, but by then they had moved, or died . . . She wanted to leave—there was a daughter in Edinburgh . . ." Hassan let his voice run down, so that it dribbled away on the long sea-breeze.

"So there's furniture?" Ricky asked, after a pause.

"Yes. Everything."

Listlessly, Hassan looked down the beach, as the others watched him.

"Packages, then!" Martin called at last. "Castaways, form a pack-train."

All bent, picked up what they could carry, followed Hassan up the slope. From its top, they could see the lie and fall of the island better. The path before them swung to the left to avoid a low spur of swelling ground, partly covered by stunted bushes. Just beyond the spur, the path divided, one route carrying on towards the coast—the southern coast, as Ricky enlightened them—while the other swung to the right and out of sight. About half a mile to the right, they could see the fold of land which marked Lachan's one stream, the source of their water. At the island's far extremity, about four miles away—"It's about four miles by five, if you take the longest bits," Hassan expounded as they walked—they could see how the land seemed to lift to a point, a sort of miniature mountain beyond which, they knew, were the cliffs they had seen from the sea.

"It's odd," Martin said, a little out of breath under his load. "To be this close to the sea, to have it all round you like this— it feels almost dangerous."

"Claustrophobic?" Ricky asked.

"Yes. Almost oppressive. That's right."

Hassan said, "An oasis in reverse," and smiled. "Because the desert waits too, it pushes at you like this, it dares you not to take it seriously . . ."

"You're both depressing me," Ricky said curtly, and followed them up the right-hand fork.

The path curved along the floor of a wide and shallow valley. To the right of them, the stunted bushes rustled in the wind; to the left, the land rose bare, then craggy, towards the blunt peak of the island. In front of them, at first faintly below the diminishing sound of the surf and then more and more clearly as they approached, they could hear the rush and clatter of the stream.

The valley narrowed briefly, to set low walls of red rock on either side of them, fronded with the green and brown of fern. Then the land opened, the path swung abruptly to the left, and they could see the stream itself, a bridge that spanned it, with on either side of this a low, grey-stone cottage.

"Home at last," Martin cried, and ran the last few strides to the stream's edge, his load leaping on his shoulders. He put it down on the mossed planks of the bridge, put one hand on the trembling rail and stared about him. He felt frightened, not knowing what would happen, uncertain whether they were really in danger. Where was Melton? How had he reacted to their disappearance? He shivered, then turned, smiling.

"A domain," he said. "A Walden. My friends, we have come back to Nature, that great Mother from whose side we strayed so long ago . . ."

"Don't mock it," Ricky said, but smiled.

"Mock! I pour out the central truths of my heart and you think it mockery?"

"It'll have its revenge—it's deep and devious and it's been here longer than we have."

"A pantheist! Did you imagine that, Hassan?"

"Ripe to play goddess, perhaps," Hassan said, his voice suddenly harsh, so that what he said sounded almost like an insult.

Martin, silenced, looked at him, then in brief concern at Ricky. Finally he sighed, spread his right arm in an attenuated gesture taking in the stream, the cottages and the hills.

"Explain all this, then," he demanded of Hassan. "Is this the centre of the island?"

Ricky came to stand beside him on the bridge. Hassan kept a little distance from them. He said, "This is almost the centre of the island. Just below us, about a couple of hundred yards, there is a sort of pool where the stream opens out for a bit. One can swim there, I seem to remember; that leaves the water here for drinking."

"It can be taken, then?" Martin asked.

"Yes. Just a drop in a bucket . . . About four hundred yards upstream there is another pool, and beyond that the stream is

132

much narrower and faster—it comes down from just below the mountain up there. On the other side of the peak—perhaps we shall call it The Peak, in memory of the holiday we did not have—" and he smiled ferociously, "on the other side and along the whole of that coast, there are cliffs—nearly two hundred feet high below The Peak itself. The rest of the coast is pretty bumpy too, even where there are no cliffs—you can see that there is a whole line of hills there running down from The Peak, and they curl right round the west and the north of Lachan; then there is a short gap where the coast is rocky, then the low hillocks we have just come over, and of course that beach where we landed—that is the only beach there is. After that it is low cliffs and rocky coast and points and caps and sharp little bays right round to The Peak and the cliffs again."

"Homey. Sounds more like Alcatraz," Martin murmured.

"But it's beautiful!" Ricky disagreed.

"I know." Martin laughed. "If we redefine freedom as solitude, which is perhaps as it should be, we're wilder than the birds out here."

Hassan looked elsewhere. He felt tense, yet somehow at a great distance from himself. He walked with the other two, spoke to them, answered when they spoke to him, but lived in some dimension in which they had no place. If he had been able to take in Martin's chatter about solitude, he would have smiled; he felt marooned in a loneliness so profound that he had not yet properly recognised it. Only if someone had been able to penetrate it would he have understood how complete and total it had become. As it was, he only knew that the voices he heard seemed to come from far away, faintly and almost without meaning, that the place he stood in was the same as any other place in which he might have been, almost lost behind the superimposed geography of his imagination.

He said, "We will have to choose which cottage belongs to whom." He glanced at the sky, its late-afternoon glow already tainted by the first corrupting stains of night. "After dark, it will be difficult for us."

"And there's wood to be got, for hot water," Ricky pointed out.

"And soup," Martin added. "Hot soup for the pioneers."

"All right, then," Hassan said, in a tight, controlled voice the others had never heard him use. "Which cottage?"

"Which?" Martin asked Ricky.

"Well, there are two of us—I think that one is the larger." She pointed across the stream to the cottage that stood there, backed against rocks and fern.

"Right." Martin picked up his package. "We claim transpontine Lachan. All right?"

Hassan nodded and without a word walked towards the grey house that stood, sagging-roofed, on his side of the stream. Ricky hesitated, looking after him for a moment before shrugging and hurrying off across the bridge.

"Marvellous," Martin said, having walked through the cottage's two rooms. "Look at that furniture—made to withstand hurricane and the millennia . . ."

"Huge bed," Ricky murmured.

"Enormous," Martin agreed. "I'll be able to get away from you at last."

"Poor creature, ceaselessly importuned by desperate women."

"One woman—even if she seems legion."

"I hope the sheets won't be mildewed."

He nodded. "Smells a bit damp."

"They're in this chest . . . I wonder when they were used last."

And Ricky began the swift rituals of settling in, while Martin carried what she needed to the places where she wanted it, then set it down. He fetched blankets, tinned food, water from the stream.

After a while she said, "We need wood."

Martin stood in the open doorway and looked at her. He felt reluctant to leave her alone. Across the bridge there seemed no sort of movement; perhaps Hassan was locked in, settled behind closed doors and windows, brooding on his nebulous grievances against the world. If Ricky stayed without protection, would he move, would he step with some preposterous demand from his world into theirs?

"Something wrong?" Ricky asked.

"Wrong?"

"You're staring at me, you don't seem able to speak . . . I only asked you to fetch a little wood for a fire."

"Yes." Martin sighed, stretched. It was soon for Hassan to

move. He too perhaps would want the island's strangeness to pass. And it may be that his fears of those who menaced him had weakened his own impulse to attack; after all, he had fought side by side with Ricky and Martin, they had all three been comrades in arms. Certainly Hassan had not been unfriendly during their drive across the north; he had been taciturn, but human, had smiled at times, chatted a little over meals, spoken once of his dead mother.

"Yes," Martin said again. "I think I'll have time to get wood."

"Time?"

"Well, evening . . . it's a quick dusk, I expect, up here."

"Wrong. It's long and slow. There's a hatchet and a saw in that box in the kitchen."

"Right!"

Passing Hassan's cottage, Martin watched for some sign, a movement by a window, a closing door. But no sound came; the cottage seemed derelict. Martin smiled, probably Hassan, overcome by the rigours of the recent crossing, was fast asleep. He walked on towards the scrub that covered the hillside, swinging his saw and his hatchet like some super-confident Crusoe about to tame a wilderness. Ricky, humming as she hurried, washed crockery and cutlery, piled blankets on the bed, swept the wooden floors, cleaned the two small windows, set their toothbrushes in mugs beside the sink, ordered the tins they had brought in bright rows on the cupboard shelves, scrubbed the deal top of the kitchen table.

From the doorway, Hassan said, "Ricky!"

She turned, smiling consciously, determined on politeness. His voice was still toneless, a little hoarse; she wondered why his manner had changed.

"Something isn't working?" she asked. "You need help? There's no water? The sheets are damp? Torn? Non-existent? . . ."

"We must settle things," Hassan said, abruptly. He came into the cottage and as the light from the window beside the sink fell on his face Ricky saw that he was sweating.

"Settle things?"

"I am not to be laughed at. I am not to be disregarded, turned away . . ."

"I don't know what you're talking about. It's not those people

135

again?"

Facing each other, they seemed hemmed in by the island's silence, by the endless sound of the reaching sea beyond.

Hassan said in a low voice, "It must be settled."

"What must be settled? In what way settled?"

Ricky tried to stand straight, to speak coolly, but her voice shook, she felt weak; perhaps she would cry, or vomit. Hassan, facing her, stared past her eyes, his gaze fixed; he might have been listening to some distant prompting.

He said, "You think you despise me. But all that is nonsense. If you once understand the power I carry, the strength I have . . . who I am; if you once understand who I am . . . You must realise that it is a question of who one is, of worthiness. Death carries its rewards; there are rewards for the dealers of death. But all that you will not understand. Only if you looked at me, if you really saw . . . Now, these hands, for example . . ."

The flat tones ceased. Hassan lifted his hands in front of him, stretched and tensed the fingers. He looked at his hands and smiled slightly.

"Death? What do you mean? Power? I don't understand you." Ricky was breathless with the first pressures of fear.

"You would not have spoken to me in the way you did if you had understood. That we must learn, we must know that. But you will. Laura made her mistake, she turned her head away, she looked elsewhere, not understanding; but you, much wiser, will not behave in the same way."

"I, wiser? But Laura's . . . Isn't it true, after all—the story about Laura, what you told us at the café, isn't it? . . ."

"But all that is over and not worth talking about; what must be settled is between us, between you and me . . ."

"There's nothing between you and me," Ricky shouted, her voice suddenly shrill. "There's nothing. I detest you and I always have. From the beginning!"

"It must be decided, you see. The question of a choice cannot enter into it. Or a choice between what I am and any other person. Because I am beyond that now, I am in a new world now —it is this person whom you shall recognise in the end . . . and nothing less."

"I don't understand the choice, the question . . ."

136

Hassan stood straighter. Ricky noticed that he was suddenly much paler; sweat stood in great drops on his forehead, rolled slowly down his smooth, round cheeks.

"It cannot be Martin. This is a question of sense. He will discard you. But that is beside the point. It cannot be Martin because I must be the man." His breathing was shorter now; he almost panted out the words. "I have said there are houses. I have said there is money. But all that is nothing to do with it. Because I am who . . . what I am, you must end all this, you must take the gifts I have."

"You're mad!" Ricky cried.

There was a long pause after this. Only Hassan's breathing lay between them; he sounded like a man desperately afraid.

"You must stay with me. From now on."

"But you know that's impossible."

"You must stay with me, you must share my roof. I will not submit to this indignity."

"And Martin?" Ricky asked, shrilly. "And him—what'll happen to him?"

"That is the simple point. I will kill Martin. It is for that reason that I am stronger; it is then you will understand what I am."

"You will? . . . What will you? . . ."

Ricky stared, her muscles giving way, energy fleeing. She thought she would fall.

Hassan said, "You have to understand that killing is easy. That is the first thing. And someone killed is . . . dead. That is the second thing. There are no further consequences. It has a purity that . . . The hands move, you see; then there is a result of that movement. After that, new things begin."

"I haven't understood you?" Ricky moaned. She moved backwards until the stained draining-board supported her. "It isn't the truth . . . all that? I mean, the way you're talking, the things you're saying . . ."

"I no longer have to lie to you. That is part of the point. You are beginning to understand my strength, my worth."

"You said . . . you said, as for Martin . . . You said you'd . . ."

"Kill. Yes. The word is easy—as easy as the action. The hands will do it, if asked. Or even before—without question or order

137

". . . But all that is beside the point."

"You'd kill Martin?"

"Yes. For my need, and for you. Of course."

He moved towards her and she screamed. He put his hand out, but timidly. She moved away and screamed again. He frowned.

"No," he muttered. "No. You must agree. To disagree . . . I would not put up with that."

Ricky turned, ran for the door.

"No!" Hassan shouted. He trapped her right arm, just below the shoulder, swung her round. She fell into a chair, stumbled, slipped sideways. The chair fell and the sudden sound unsettled Hassan, so that for a moment his grasp of her weakened. Pulling herself free, rolling across the stone floor of the kitchen, Ricky tried to get further from him.

"No," Hassan said again. "No. After all this time, there cannot be any way to disappoint me."

He pushed the chair aside, bent towards her. She screamed again, scrambling back.

"You must not move!" Hassan shouted. "You must not move away! You have to understand that."

But Ricky no longer heard him. The light that flowed in from the open door was all that she was conscious of; the day would embrace her, in that air she would be able to breathe.

Hassan bent, dragged her towards him by her waist; her knees scraped across the floor. She ducked her head, hunched her shoulders for protection. Hassan raised his right hand, struck at her as she tried to pull free. His hand caught her left shoulder; the very force of the blow knocked her further from him, so that cloth, tearing, left him with no more than a few red strands from her dress in his left hand.

She, sobbing, crawled towards the light. Off balance, Hassan reached for her, but she threw herself forward and his lunge missed. Then she was on her feet, staggering forward, lurching through the door into the brightness.

"Martin! Martin!" But her voice was choked, without force or direction. Behind her she heard Hassan call after her. She ran towards the bridge; as she reached its far side, she heard his feet hit the wooden floor. She strained, running past the other cottage, hearing Hassan behind her, searching through the blurring of tears for Martin.

But the footsteps behind her veered away. Dimly, she heard the door of Hassan's cottage flung open. She looked briefly over her shoulder. He was no longer following. Bewildered, she hesitated for a moment, then put her head down and ran on.

"Martin," she called, "Martin."

But when Martin, hurrying towards her, axe in hand, caught her by a wide-flung wrist, she screamed. She had been shouting his name unaware; now, looking dazedly up at him, she hardly recognised who held her. Her head against his chest, she began to sob, the sound dry and hard as, at the same time, she struggled to get her breath back.

"Hassan," she said, over and over. "Hassan. Hassan."

"What about him? God, I didn't think . . . So soon! Where is he?"

"Mad. Mad. It was him . . . the other time . . . Must have been."

"Where is he now?"

"He . . . he said he'd kill . . . kill you. He said he'd . . . And he hit me, attacked me—it was like the other time. It must have been him. Hit me, hit me . . . tried to get hold of me, hurt me . . ."

"I shouldn't have left you alone. I knew I shouldn't have gone."

"He came to the cottage. He attacked me. He said he'd kill you."

"Me!"

"Talked of it, of killing; as if he . . . Martin, he's mad. Is, or gone, has always been—I don't know. But . . ."

"Oh, if it's that, if it's a fight . . ."

His fist tight about the haft of the axe, Martin pushed her to one side, began to trot down the path towards the cottages.

"No," Ricky called, half-blind with weeping, "no, he means it. He's mad. Don't go there. Please, Martin."

She began to follow, her hands making small, stiff gestures of pleading. Once she tripped and nearly fell; in this way the distance between her and Martin widened.

Something fell, breaking sharply. The sound split momentarily the island's silence. Turning the bend that led to the cottages Ricky saw the axe lying across the path and Martin rolling behind scrub and fern.

"Get down," he shouted. "Down!"

She stood, stupidly, not understanding what she saw or heard. "For Christ's sake, get down!" Martin yelled. "He's got the gun!"

Then she saw Hassan. He was running along the edge of the stream, his right hand held awkwardly in front of him. Above the bunched fingers, metal gleamed. As she watched, he veered from the water, climbed the low slope on the other side of the path. The metal in his hand was lifted, held higher. Again, the sudden cleaving of silence. To her right, something—an insect? A thrown stone?—hummed through the tops of the ferns. Seagulls and guillemots screamed above the cliffs behind her.

"He's shooting!" she shouted. "He's going to kill us."

She ran to her left, stumbling through fern and low bushes, her feet slipping on generations of rotting leaves. Beside her, Martin suddenly appeared. Again there was the sound of the gun; at the same second, Martin had thrown her sideways, so that both of them went sprawling.

Hassan stood crouched on the opposite slope. He looked down at the pistol in his hands, his lips thin with fury. He had wasted his advantage, his surprise; he had been too eager. He should have let Martin come close to him; instead, he had been careless, too involved; and so had shot too soon. As he had at Ricky, at this girl who had refused him, who had refused to understand, turning away, screaming, to find sanctuary in the arms of her feeble lover. But all that would change, strength and weakness would be demonstrated.

"I will kill you!" he shouted suddenly. Sending out his challenge and decree in this way made him feel better. "I will kill you! I will kill you!"

He hurried down the slope towards the path below him. He watched the far side of the shallow valley, trying to see from the shaking of vegetation where these frightened people were, hiding or crawling out of sight into what they imagined would be safety. But the bright wind from the sea crossed and crisscrossed the low hills, sending branches and heather and fern-tips shivering now this way, now that. Bemused, Hassan waited on the path; then, like a casting hound, began a series of cautious zig-zags to flush out what he hunted.

"We've got a chance," Martin whispered. "If we sit absolutely still, there's a chance."

They were in a tangled hollow, ramparted by roots, roofed by dead and sagging branches. Above these, leaves rattled in the breeze, dark green against the pale blue of the sky.

"He won't see us until he's close—if he sees us at all. But we'll see him."

He looked through the pattern of grass and branches, searching for Hassan, listening for the patterned sigh and crunch of his footsteps. He felt incongruously released. It's begun, he thought. Finally, he's in the open.

"Whatever you do, sit still, make no sound, no move," he breathed. "No move."

Black against brightness, the crouched back, the thrust-forward head of Hassan. Ricky let out a gasp of fear, then compressed her lips, buried her face in the dank soil beneath her. Martin curled and uncurled his fingers; only now he remembered the axe and where and when he had dropped it. Without a weapon, he would have small chance—but a chance, all the same. If he could erupt out of this hiding place, burst on Hassan before the gun could swing round, the finger squeeze that trigger . . . He glanced at his own hands, watched their trembling, listened to his shallow, frightened breathing. He licked dry lips; would he be too scared to move when the time came?

Hassan halted. To Martin, below ground level, he seemed tall as a giant. Fee fi fo fum . . . And indeed he stared about him, he seemed to sniff the air, as if he knew his quarry was within reach. Slowly Hassan turned. Martin could see the sudden glint as light struck his eyes, the gun he carried. He could see Hassan's deep frown. Beside him, Ricky trembled; he felt the shudders that raked her body.

Hassan took a step up the slope, stood level with the hollow now, hesitated; then walked further. Martin relaxed. He thought he might cry. With an unsteady hand, he brushed hair off his forehead.

"Has he gone?" Ricky whispered.

"For the moment."

Not moving, they waited, starting as birds crashed to shelter in nearby branches, as sudden winds flung twigs into unexpected dance. They saw Hassan twice more, once running diagonally down the slope, and then, half an hour later, standing on the opposite side of the valley. This time Hassan was shouting. Martin could not hear what the words were, because the rising evening wind flung them off Hassan's lips sideways to the sea. But he knew they were threats.

They sat silently, close together, through the blue-grey evening. Martin had both arms about Ricky, partly to soothe her, partly to keep the two of them warm. Low clouds thinned and broke to let pale moonlight through. Stars sat in the sky's clearings, from time to time obscured by the tattered clouds. The sea hammered at the rocks along the island's southern shore; the cry and spread of waves seemed a base of sound for the night to rest on.

.   .   .

Five hundred miles away, Detective-Superintendent Melton said, "All right. They ate in Carlisle. Yesterday. But we need to be a hell of a lot more up-to-date than that. Or else we've lost them."

Harroway cleared his throat, sighed. "Well, now we do know they crossed the Pennines . . ."

"And went north or doubled back?"

"I don't know, sir."

"No. None of us knows."

"Except that Burani's got enemies—judging from that fight."

Melton shrugged. "All right. But what are those three up to? Prescott and the girl aren't Burani's bosom pals . . ."

"According to them, sir."

"Yes. According to them, And if they're not, what are they doing, running round the country harnessed up like some damned troika? And where the hell are they going?"

After a pause, Harroway said, "If Prescott's really straight, sir, I suppose he might have felt he had to stick to Burani until we'd caught up."

"That's what I'm hoping—though hope isn't perhaps the exact sentiment. Because, if it's true, we'd better catch up bloody quick."

He stared blank-faced at Harroway, then gave a short, aggressive nod. He said, "I want them to give this one the works."

"Yes. Priority. Countrywide?"

"That's right. Countrywide."

.　　　.　　　.

"It's dark," Ricky said. The silence between them had lasted over two hours.

"Yes," Martin agreed, and rocked her slowly to and fro, as if she were a child. "Yes, it's night."

"He's mad, isn't he?"

"Hassan? Yes. I imagine he is."

"He wanted to marry me . . . wanted me to go off with him, in any case. I thought he had a girl."

"She was at that party. You saw her. That party where they met again."

"Yes, I saw her." Ricky paused, then seemed to sink even more closely into Martin's warmth. "Perhaps he killed her."

"Laura?"

"Yes. Perhaps he killed her, like he tried to kill me."

"Perhaps."

"What'll we do now?"

Martin shrugged. "I don't know. Maybe I could swim. But I don't want to leave you alone."

She shook her head. "No. In any case it's miles—twelve, they said, to the mainland. And there are currents, and the cold . . . No, that's no solution."

Martin considered his duty—to Ricky, to the police. But Melton might be anywhere, might have lost their trail for ever.

"We must get off," he said.

Ricky thought for a moment, then said in a bleak voice, "We can't."

"Can't?"

"Well, how can we? How would we do it?"

"There's no old boat, nothing we could float again?"

"How would we find it? Anyway, he told us that was the only beach."

"No way to make a signal?"

"None that Hassan wouldn't see before anyone else."

Martin grunted, looked down at Ricky. "We'll have to wait out the week, then," he said very slowly. "Till the boat comes back."

Ricky said nothing for a while, then shivered, muttered, "I'm cold."

"Yes. So'm I. We'll have to do something about that."

"We can't make a fire."

"No. And we can't stay here. He'll look here in the morning. In any case, it's too close to the cottages."

"Oh, that bloody Hassan," Ricky said, suddenly. "Bloody, bloody Hassan . . . You've worked so hard, you've done so well—and we've waited so long; and now . . ."

"If we survive, it'll make a fine story."

"It won't make a bad one, even if we don't."

"'Madman slays Two on Island Hideout.' You're right—it's full of promise."

They laughed in a small, strained sort of way, but then felt a little better.

"We'll have to get blankets," Martin said.

"And food—something, anyway."

"Yes. We'll have to think."

It was an hour or so later that they slipped out of their sheltered hollow and crept up through the long fern to the wind-clipped top of the low ridge. Once they were the far side of this, they moved silently and yard by yard across the night, following the line of this spur of the higher hills behind them, until they reached the point where the ground fell away towards the endless clatter of the stream.

"Upper Pool's just here," Ricky whispered.

Martin nodded. "Then his cottage is just to the right of us, and the bridge just beyond that."

"Yes."

"You can get across the pool?"

"Of course."

Dry-lipped, she kissed him on the cheek, then slid away down the steep slope. Martin waited, tensed to shout, to stand and run, crouching, towards gunfire or challenge. But the shadows that hid the cottages remained undisturbed. He heard a soft splash as Ricky stepped into the shallow water, saw from above the pool her shadow bar for a moment the thin, reflected moonlight. He stared about him, listened with an intensity he would only a day before have thought impossible; but there was no sign of Hassan. He glanced at his watch, then began in his turn to move down the hill, keeping the stream to the left of him, following it by its sound.

As Ricky approached it she could see the still, low bulk of their cottage. She lay still, watched it for a long time. No sound came from it, no light, no movement. She felt very concentrated and, although her breathing was swift and shallow, she was no longer conscious of fear. Pulling herself forward on her elbows, careful of stones and twigs, she approached the building, one slow inch after another. Still there was silence.

When the walls of the cottage were above her like cliffs, fear suddenly returned. Shadows swam together to make a crouched Hassan, the sound of the nearby stream translated into a madman's laughter, the blackness of the house was no more than a cover for ambush, for incipient murder. She lay, trembling, an offered victim for a meaningless sacrifice. But no bullet came, no voice, no sudden hand out of the night to hold her. Very slowly she stood up, leaned against the rough stones of the cottage. Her legs trembled uncontrollably and for a moment she closed her eyes. She felt very hot. Her throat felt dry and constricted as she panted in terror.

She clenched her fists, trying to force herself to move; like someone on a cliff face, she seemed unable to take another step. But the step had to be taken. She bent, picked up a stone.

Hassan sat beside the bridge. The gun lay in his lap. He stared in front of him. He waited. He had been trained for this, he was on his own battlefield, the night was his parish. When the glass of the window in the cottage smashed and fell with a sound like suddenly arrested sleighbells, he smiled. As he had foreseen, hunger had brought his quarry to him. He stood, quite slowly, then ran noiselessly across the bridge.

Outside the cottage he halted. Cautiously he approached the door, listened. There was no sound from inside. He bit his lip thoughtfully, then lay flat, crawled to the corner of the building. No one was there, although above him the broken window glittered in the faint starlight. He smiled, turned and in one movement stood up and crashed through the door. His right hand found the light switch, he shut his eyes tightly, then opened them. The kitchen was empty. To his left was the open window.

"I know you are here," he said.

He waited, then leaped for the far door, tugged it open, then jumped back. No one came out, no one stood within.

"You are hiding," he said. "I will find you. You cannot beat me, because I am trained. Come out!"

No one answered, nothing moved.

He stepped forward, then threw himself flat, rolled through the doorway, came lithely to his feet, the pistol high. The room was empty.

Martin heard the fall of glass when he was three-quarters of the way down the slope towards the cottages. The sound reached him across the burbling of water, cutting sharply through this and the sighing night. He slowed, to move forward even more cautiously than before. If he heard it, so had Hassan; in a moment, the darkness could change from shelter to trap.

He was within sight of Hassan's cottage—a black oblong against the low, charcoal hills—when he saw the light go on in the other building across the stream. He watched the swift silhouette that was Hassan leap across the doorway, then out of sight. He began to run.

The door to Hassan's cottage was unlocked. Martin pushed it open. He could see, his eyes now accustomed to blackness, that the floor in front of him was littered with objects. For a moment he was puzzled, then slowly smiled to himself: Hassan had brought everything out of the other cottage, the better to guard it. Martin bent, began to work. He found a pile of blankets and spread one of these out. He threw two other blankets in it, then two loaves of bread, a bottle of milk, a box of Camembert, a tin of pâté, a tin of ham, a jar of olives, a salami, a knife and a tin opener; he flung the corners of the opened blanket together, twisted and knotted them, his fingers struggling frantically to make what he had gathered safe. He was aware of the open door behind him; the skin of his back crawled with fear. As he worked, he could already hear the sudden, final detonation that might at any moment come at him out of the night.

Hassan ran through the kitchen of the other cottage, put out the light, then dived head first through the door. But no one had been waiting to attack him, crouched against the wall beside the doorjamb. He rose, stood still, listened. To his right, a bush rustled and he swung round, strained eyes and ears; in a moment he heard it again.

146

Ricky, on the slope above him, could see a nebulous darkness—all she could make out of Hassan—start to climb. She turned, moved quietly over the ridge, to the fold of land that lay beyond it, before the slow rise of the land towards the escarpments that lay above Lachan's western shore. Once out of sight of the cottages, she turned to her left, began to run. After a moment or so she veered to her right, threw herself down in thick fern and heather, then lay still.

Hassan, now on the ridge, peered through the darkness. In all directions bushes, wind-shaken, distracted him. Two or three times he thought he heard someone move, so that, pistol ready, he swung round to face attack. But the night remained empty, innocent. He began to run along the top of the ridge, not yet prepared to admit that he was moving aimlessly. When he arrived on the slopes above the Upper Pool, he stopped.

"I will kill you!" he shouted. "Kill you both!"

He turned, wide eyes on a moving branch; it tossed again and he pulled the trigger. The noise thrust across the silence; leaves and bark flew ineffectually; then night, stillness, the endless distant sibilance of waves, closed over the moment as if to heal a wound.

Ricky heard him call and shoot. The sound was very close and she cowered nearer to the ground. She waited, staring towards the place from which the noise and the report had come.

"The island is small," Hassan screamed. "I have days yet—days! I will show you strength. I will show you that I have strength." He paused, then shouted again. "Ricky! Ricky! I am the stronger. You will understand. But all that will be too late. Because both of you . . . both of you, now; I will kill you both!"

She heard him run back along the ridge. For a moment she thought she saw him against the dying moonlight and the stars. She waited to hear if he would come back, then slowly, carefully, she stood up. Crouched down, ready to fall flat, to turn, to hide, even to scream or weep, to beg, if necessary, she ran under the ridge's shadow towards the stream.

Above Upper Pool she hesitated. The water gleamed faintly. Anyone lying there would see her move when she crossed. But she had to get to the other side. She took a deep breath, then careered down the slope, jumping now and then to avoid rocks or bushes, terrified that at any moment she might fall, yet more terrified now of stopping, of staying in the place where Hassan only moments before had stood to bellow his threats.

The water was icy cold as she began to cross. She found that, hurrying, hunched, towards the other side, she was sobbing in terror.

"Please," she heard herself say, over and over again. "Please, please . . ."

The dark slopes behind and in front appeared to close in, to be moving towards each other like vast, destructive jaws. And at any moment that high voice would scream its commands out of the darkness, the thudding pistol would send bullets like the insects of death humming across the night.

But Lachan stayed silent. On the far shore of the pool she dropped to her knees, remained like that for long moments, her head hanging in exhaustion. Then, slowly, she began to climb the other side of the valley.

"You!"

Martin whispered this, kneeling between two bushes. Ricky gasped, then ran towards him. She dropped her head against his chest and began convulsively to weep.

"I can't," she said, her voice harsh through tears. "I can't do it."

"Yes, you can. You just did." Martin laughed, patted her shoulder. "Come on. We're soldiers now."

She looked up at him, frowning, pushing away tears. "You're enjoying this," she said.

"No. That's too strong—but there's something . . . It's simplicity, this. Life here, death there. And everything up to us. And you to protect and help. It's as if all sorts of bits and pieces in my life had come together—while all the rest had dropped away, dropped off; useless, frills I never really needed . . . But come on; we can't stay here."

She nodded and looked around her. "We'll go on up the valley."

He bent and picked up the knotted blanket. She frowned.

"It worked, then."

"Of course."

She shrugged. "I'd forgotten." She began to laugh, though a little bitterly. "I was so frightened, so worried about myself . . ."

148

"It worked very sweetly. When the glass broke he must have shuffled over there at once."

"He didn't stay in the cottage long; when he came out, I waved a couple of branches at him."

"It fetched him?"

"Hound to scent. Then he ran along that ridge opposite. And yelled and screamed."

"Something horrible. I heard him."

She shuddered. "It wasn't really funny. I was too close. Then he loosed off that shot and ran back."

Martin laughed. "When I heard how far away he was, I decided to go in for a bit of sabotage. I ripped up his bread, I threw water over all his blankets, I emptied as many tins as I could find on the floor . . . Marvellous, altogether."

"But you brought with you . . ."

"As much as I could carry." He laughed down at her, then bent and kissed her cheek. "Come on. You be the guide—so guide us somewhere."

They began to walk along the southern slope of the valley, climbing slowly. Now and again the tins in the blanket Martin carried clanked softly together. The stream straggled beside them, getting quieter as it narrowed into a ditch-like brook. It hissed down a low cliff-face, then forked.

"We'll cross here," Ricky said in a low voice. She took Martin's hand and led him across the stream's southern fork. Between the two halves of the divided stream, the ground rose softly, leading with increasing steepness to the highest points of the island.

"We climb?" Martin asked.

"Highest is safest," Ricky replied. "We ought at least to be able to see him coming."

Side by side, they walked up the hillside. Once Martin rested, throwing his improvised pack on the ground and sitting beside it. She flung herself full-length, looked up at him.

"Do you think he's following us?" he asked.

"I don't think so. We've left the stream now—we'd have heard him."

They sat without speaking, listening into the night. But there came back to them only a sense of emptiness, of the loneliness of sea and rock and darkness. After a while, still without a word, they stood up, continued their climb.

The Peak itself was rounded, wind-bitten. Here and there rock outcropped darkly. Ricky led Martin to the left, so that they went round the last shoulder of the hill. A few moments walking brought them to the edge of the cliffs. Just to the right of them was the island's southern tip. Below, the sea cast and clattered among the rocks and shale, as if it were alive and searching. They could see the occasional flash of foam as waves turned over or retreated from some saw-tooth of stone. The wind, which was south-westerly, struck them sharply in the face.

Ricky took Martin's hand. Slowly they followed an almost faded path that led along the cliff-edge. Below them, the point of the island struck out at the sea in a litter of monumental rocks.

"Where are we going?" Martin asked. "They should signpost these places."

"There must be something where the cliff-face breaks up."

Ricky tugged at his hand, and he followed as she began to climb once more. Here the land rose very steeply, lifting to The Peak almost as an extension of the cliffs below. Bent double, reaching with their spread hands, they scrambled higher.

"I'll look over there—I'm lighter than you are," Ricky said. She began to traverse the slope, moving to her right. Martin, behind her, felt the wind tug at what he carried. He stopped, half-yawning. He watched the crab-like shape of Ricky moving on. Then shadow swallowed her.

"Come on!"

He climbed towards her voice. Suddenly the rocky hillside slid into itself. Darkness lay in a pool, like lava in a crater.

Out of this, "Quickly!" Ricky whispered. He stepped forward, suddenly on nearly level ground.

"A cave," he said. "You were right."

Martin walked from side to side of the narrow cleft in the rocks. Outside, the wind hummed across the cliffs, but here they were sheltered from it. The sea below sighed and murmured, and somewhere behind them there was the irregular dripping of water.

"What time is it?" Ricky asked.

Martin glanced at the luminous hands of his watch, then laughed. "I thought it'd be four in the morning. It's just after midnight."

He bent, untied his pack. He set the tins on the ground, laid the bread across them, the other things beyond. Then he spread the blankets, doubled, across the floor.

"One of us'll have to watch."

Ricky sighed. "Yes. Who?"

"You sleep. I'll see how long I can manage. Then I'll wake you. We can work out what we'll do tomorrow."

He put his arms round her and she said, "We've got days of this yet. Days."

"We'll manage."

"How?"

"Like tonight. Because there are two of us. By intelligence. With a bit of luck, with luck."

She shivered again, rubbed her cheek against his jersey.

She said, "You can't really be confident."

"No. Not confident. But we've managed this evening."

"Yes. We have." She nodded, then lay down, pulled the blankets over her shoulders.

"Here, like this, I'm totally involved with you," he said.

"I love you," she answered, simply.

"Yes," he said. "That's how we'll manage."

She sighed, moving her head in a slow, half-hidden nod. A moment later, she was asleep.

Martin sat just inside the cave's entrance. He breathed deeply, watching the night. The wind fluttered the dry grass, then hurled itself in charging gusts at the peak above. He wondered at his new-found peace. He should have been excited, frightened, undecided. Instead he felt almost happy; certainly fatalistically prepared for whatever was to come during the next few days.

I should tell Ricky the truth, he thought; then shook his head. It would be almost sadistic to give her false hope: only Melton could rescue them and where was he? The McLeods' boat would be coming back in a week, but what would a couple of off-guard fishermen be able to do against an armed and determined, a lunatic Hassan? No, there was nothing to be said, no notion of Melton in pursuit to be held out for them to cling to— they were on their own. If they were to survive now, it would be because of their own efforts.

I'm doing what I should, he thought, peering across the darkness. There's danger, a woman to protect . . . Ricky to protect; it makes sense of what we feel for each other, of what I feel for her.

"Which is?" he asked aloud.

He looked back at the indistinct shape of her sleeping, blanket-covered body. Perhaps the simplicities of their situation here were as misleading as the complexities of town. He shook his head. The chances of death altered who they were on Lachan; in face of a threat so direct, some alteration would be expected, some adjustment of the mind and the emotions; he would never be the same again.

"Yet how changed?"

He nodded wisely out towards the cliff, but came to no easy conclusion. It might be that he had parted company with emotion, with sentiment; that the peace he felt now, the sense that he could accept whatever might occur, would lead him not towards Ricky but away, not towards other people, relationships, a joining of lives, but in the opposite direction.

Yet he felt very sharp, very concentrated. He had focused his concern on Ricky, had limited the scope of his energy and intelligence to her protection, to their joint survival. Would that not continue? Had he not reduced his vision of himself, thus drawing in ambition to these fundamentals? And had he not at the same time grown more certain, stronger? Had not the complex, image-bedevilled elsewhere brought him to lies and self-delusion?

"But I won that prize. I have a career," he argued. Until that moment, that winning, he himself had often thought that he was living in dreams, using the picture of himself that he presented —of a young, aspiring architect rich with ideas and visions and potential—as no more than a screen to keep him from the realities of life. And from its obligations, such as his emotional responsibilities for Ricky.

"But I kept faith," he muttered to himself, nodding again. "I made myself promises and kept them."

"Myself," he thought; what sort of word was that? Hadn't there been other promises, made or implied? Would these too be kept?

He frowned. His self-censoring was going too far, too fast. He was in the grip of this place and this danger. It was no good coming to conclusions at such a time: later he might reverse them and that would be bad for morale. What had to be done, about his life and his ambitions and who he was and how that who would connect with Ricky, would have to be decided elsewhere, at a different time; at a moment of calm, not under stress.

"But you are calm," he told himself. Did he not feel at peace? And if he did, wasn't this a good time to . . .

All the same, the situation was unique, terrifying. It was no time to consider . . .

But when better than now, right up against the realities of life and death?

He hadn't absorbed these yet, though. Later, when he had made sense of them . . .

How would he ever? Who had ever done so to anyone's permanent satisfaction?

He frowned, staring left and right as though ready to welcome intrusion and attack. He felt bewildered. It was years since he had thought about himself, considered abstract problems rather than those which faced him in his work. Now he felt bewildered, uneasy. What was happening to him? For a practical man, he was being a bit airy-fairy, wasn't he?

But these things had to be thought out, after all. That's what being human meant. Didn't it?

Caught in this roundabout of the mind, Martin let himself be whirled across the hours. It was the long grey of dawn that checked him. Slowly, to the left of him the sky grew pinkish, then yellow, finally white. Seabirds cut, screaming, across the light. The horizon lay black and endless in his vision, then was caught by the brightness and little by little disappeared. The sun leaped from hiding.

"You didn't wake me," Ricky murmured from behind him.

He turned, smiling, and as he did so, yawned enormously.

"And look how tired you are," she added solicitously.

"I got trapped by introspection."

"I don't remember that among the military virtues."

"I'd no idea military virtue was something you'd studied." Martin smiled down at her, then crossed to where he'd left the bread. "Breakfast?"

He opened the tin of ham, cut off hunks of bread, knocked the top off the bottle of homogenised milk; side by side they sat opposite the brightening sky and wordlessly took food.

Finally Ricky sat back, asked, "What now?"

"Now?"

Martin looked about him as if the present had become an impenetrable mystery.

Ricky said, "He'll be looking for us—soon, if not yet."

Martin looked at her, nodding thoughtfully. "Soon, if not yet," he repeated slowly. He glanced at his watch. "It's six o'clock, more or less. What if he hasn't begun yet?"

"Well?"

Martin stood up, went to the cave's mouth, stared down at the cliff and the swirling water below. He said, "If we had the guts, we could . . . Look, what would make us safe on this island?"

"Getting off it," Ricky answered promptly.

"If we can't?"

"Well, if Hassan would get back sanity. Or if he . . ."

"If he?"

She glanced at him, then bright-eyed looked away. "If he fell, for instance. Got trapped in some way . . . hurt. Something like that."

"Should we wait for chance, then?"

Now their eyes met in a long glance of resolution. Then Martin nodded sharply and, turning back into the small cave, folded the blankets and pushed them and the tins and provisions into the shadows.

"No point in leaving stuff about to look conspicuous," he said. "Shall we promenade?"

"A glance at the domain?"

"And a little commerce with the serfs?"

"Why not?"

But when they had climbed The Peak and walked down its far shoulder, their confidence thinned. They walked cautiously, keeping to the cover of scrub or heather, of rocks or broken ground, as much as they could. They glanced left and right, searching out the cause of every creak and rustle around them, half prepared the whole time for the sudden screamed threat and the crash of gun-fire.

Martin pointed to their left.

"Upper Pool's over there, isn't it?"

"Yes. Other side of the rise, I think. What, are you a

geographer?"

"One remains curious, even to the end," he said, sententiously. He glanced sideways, but Ricky was not smiling.

"Once we start downhill, we'll be able to see his cottage," she said.

"All right. Then it's time we divided."

Ricky went pale. "We're going to split up again?"

She shook her head, took Martin's left wrist in her right hand, held on tightly. "No. I don't think I can."

He pulled free. "You can. In any case, we've no choice."

"Why? Why haven't we? We're together. That's all we have —that we're not alone. What's the point in being separate if we? . . ."

"All we have is four hands. We're two to his one. In this situation, that's the only advantage being double gives us." Martin's voice was low, but deliberately savage. "The only way we can beat him is by being in two places at once."

There was a pause after this. Ricky hung her head, then nodded. "I'm sorry—yes, you're right." She took a deep breath. "What do we do?"

Martin glanced up at the sky, then at his watch. "Wait here," he said, then ran, bent low for safety, towards the ridge ahead. For a moment, lying flat, he was invisible to Ricky; she stood, not moving, her fists tightly clenched, until she saw him, first wriggling backwards down the slope, then turning to run back.

"He's there!" he said in an urgent voice when he had rejoined her. "He's there—he must have been on guard. He's sitting beside the door of his cottage, leaning forward on something—a table, perhaps. Is there a table?" He frowned, trying to remember.

"There was something. I expect they sat out on summer evenings, or ate there when the sun shone."

"So he's head down on the picnic table and if we move, if we move now . . . You go down there, across the stream. Below Upper Pool there are bushes, aren't there; thickets? Go through those. I'll go straight ahead. With a bit of luck I'll get him. Hit him before he wakes, lock up the arsenal . . . But if not, if it goes wrong, you must do what you did yesterday. Try and distract him, throw him off one trail to another. And if he gets me . . ."

"No!"

"He might."

"I don't want to be here alone. I can't."

"You've got twenty square miles, for Christ's sake. If you want him to screw you, go down to him now and I'll save myself trouble."

Her lips thinned. "That's filthy and you know . . ."

Martin bent, kissed her on the cheek. "So, if he gets me, keep clear of him. Now, get going!"

He watched her slipping from clump to clump of vegetation until she finally stepped out of sight. The morning seemed very empty, strangely silent. Even the sea had flattened towards calm, since the wind had dropped throughout the second half of the night. A line of tall white clouds had formed above the mainland hills to the north-east and now stood there motionless. He sighed deeply, then a second time. He felt afraid; they were precipitating crisis, the once-for-all moment from which there could be no retreat. He began to walk towards Hassan's cottage.

At the top of the ridge he lay flat, stared down the slope. He was opposite the house's corner. Beside the front door, between it and the corner, was a low table, a bench behind it. On bench and table Hassan lay sprawled, face down, his head cradled on his arms. For warmth he had wrapped himself in a light-brown blanket. He had been keeping the dew off with a grey checked cap and this had now fallen forward to shade his eyes as he slept. Martin could not see his legs, but imagined that Hassan might well have a moment's difficulty, if it should prove necessary to come round from behind the table to defend himself.

He glanced to the left, but could see no sign of Ricky. He shrugged, measured distances; in a moment he was on his feet and running.

A third of the way down the slope two lonely pines stood side by side. Martin stopped between these, his right hand clinging to the rough, red-brown bark of one tree, his left shoulder leaning against the other. He squinted to see past the stunted, low-hanging branches. Hassan had not moved.

A thicket of broom and rowans lay at the foot of the slope. Martin ran, then fell. Lying flat, he waited, catching his breath. His palms felt moist, his fingers unsteady. He was angry at these signs of weakness. Slowly he stood up, peered over the ragged bushes. Still Hassan slept. The eastern sun had not yet risen high enough to clear the glistening roof of the cottage. In the comfort of shadow, Hassan lay relaxed, spread-eagled.

Cautiously, Martin moved to his right. When the figure of the sleeping Hassan was hidden by the corner of the cottage, he pushed his way painfully and as quietly as he could through the bushes. The slope, grey and brown, thinly covered with grass and scored by the deep marks of erosion, tilted to Martin's left. He ran across it, his eyes busy as he watched at the same time for the unevenness of the ground and a sign of an awakened Hassan.

He hit the side of the cottage with a soft smack of flesh and cloth against stone. The solidity beside him gave him comfort; from that side at least there would be no surprises. He dropped on one knee, caught his breath. To his left, the slope lifted to its crown of fern. Ahead of him, about half a mile away in a straight line, lay Upper Pool. He considered the morning, listened to its quiet noises, to the distant hiss and drag of the surf. He felt strangely apart from himself, as if in a dream. He had, he felt, no business here.

Yet there was business and time it were transacted. He flopped forward, crept to the corner, slowly peered round. Sweat rolled round his eyebrows, a tribute to fear. But Hassan slept undisturbed. An early fly hummed beside his grey cap, then rose, to disappear in the bright morning. Martin swallowed, forcing himself to breathe more steadily. He rose on one knee, shuffled nearer. His right shoulder was against the sharp angle of the corner now, his right hand braced against stone. His thigh muscles tensed like a sprinter's. His eyes focused on the rounded back Hassan presented to him from this angle, its line made clumsy by the blanket he had thrown over himself. He felt the cold air sucked into his open mouth, heard the swift whisper of his breathing. Braced, he waited, as if for some signal, some reassurance; then, his head lowered, he had leaped towards danger.

"No!"

The scream unsteadied him, slowed him. Already thrusting himself forward, he faltered. So that the first bullet cut through the air in front of him, to whirl off the stone wall of the house.

"It's a trap!" Ricky's voice was high, urgent.

Martin threw himself sideways. Elsewhere, a gun hammered again, and another bullet careered off stone across the sunlight. Hassan at his table had not moved.

Hassan?

Now Martin, close enough for truth, saw the hastily flung-together blankets, stuffed with bracken and with clothes, the cap askew on the faceless bulge which made up the head. A dummy, then . . .

And Hassan, true and alive, ran laughing up the gentle rise from the stream. Martin, crouching, turned and saw him as he stopped to shoot a third time. Falling flat, Martin heard the bullet hollow out its narrow vacuum and fly on into the dawn. Reaching forward, Martin caught the trailing leg of the dummy and tugged. It fell towards him. To his left, Hassan shot again, ran nearer.

Martin rolled away, swung himself back against the wall he had started from.

"He's running in," Ricky yelled from across the stream.

The gun clattered again, but no bullets sang. Martin knew that Hassan was shooting at Ricky.

"Are you all right?" he shouted. "Ricky, did he hit you?"

"He can't see me," she called back. "Watch yourself—he's moving nearer."

Martin hesitated, then crouched. He could see nothing. The day sounded innocent, the sparse birds marking out their territory in song, the low scrub in tiny motion under the breeze.

"He's closer!" Ricky yelled.

Martin waited another second, then suddenly screamed, "Hassan!"

At the same moment, he threw out the dummy he had been holding. It came out from the side of the building with its head low and one badly stuffed arm flung wide. Ricky screamed. Nearer, Hassan loosed off three shots, the last throwing the dummy to one side like the rag it was. But Martin had gained time, a moment of diversion. He jack-knifed like a diver, flinging himself sideways, already running as the first shot from Hassan tore shreds off the dummy's head.

Ricky, on the far side of the stream, began to whoop like a Red Indian warrior. Hassan, distracted, swung momentarily towards her. She stood on the sky-line, running to her left, waving both arms like someone trying to divert a straying herd. Hassan shot in her direction, the action automatic; he knew she was out of range. Swinging back to Martin, he saw the flash of his yellow shirt as he dived for the cover of the lowest clumps of broom.

Stupidly, Hassan shouted, "You! You!" He began to scramble up the slope. Behind him, he could hear Ricky scream out her warnings. Nearer the bunched lines of ragged scrub behind which Martin had hidden, he slowed. Crouched, watchful, he closed the distance. Then, with three quick strides to his right he was past the bushes and overlooking the place where he had last seen Martin. But there was no sign of anyone. Hassan knelt, stared round him. Very carefully he watched all the plants and ridges of the hillside, examined the long shadows, the leap and flutter of birds.

Higher up, he saw a branch suddenly wave, bend, snap back into position. He shot, aiming just below the point where he had seen movement. Then, on his toes, he ran towards the bush, his gun level and aimed.

If Martin had ever been there, he had gone. Hassan dropped. Lying on his stomach, panting lightly, he felt fury surge through and about him, like an ocean in which he would drown. He stared, wildly now, to left and right. Nothing moved. He saw the two pine trees above him. Had something just stepped out of sight behind their trunks? He shot again, twice; the red-brown bark leaped and cascaded, shredding as it fell.

Hassan shouted, not able to enunciate true words, as if his anger was moving too swiftly for meaning. He felt his education, the learned calm of the killer, roll off him like sweat. He twisted to the right, got to his feet. Not concerned now with plans or caution, trapped in the currents of his frustration, he raced down towards his cottage, then veered to the left and crossed the narrow wooden bridge, his feet making a soft thunder on the dark planks.

"Ricky!" he screamed, halting for a moment, his head turning as if he were blind. "Ricky!"

The ridge above remained empty. He ran to the left, climbing diagonally. When he reached the top, he ran on, straight, not knowing where he was going. The long whips of broom slashed at his sides, heather ripped at him, here and there low creepers of bramble threatened to trip him up.

When the clear water of Upper Pool shone below him, he stopped. He turned around, then again; he was like someone about to begin a savage, hallucinating dance. A stone caught his heel and he fell heavily, rolling almost to the top of the slope that dropped to the water. There he lay, no longer able to decide on movement. Around him, the apparent emptiness of the island seemed to mock him. He moved over to lie on his back. He felt confused, unable to focus on himself. His thoughts moved slowly, heavily, always just below the threshold of understanding. Already, before he could settle them into focus, they would dissolve and disappear like half-remembered dreams.

Slowly he stood up.

"There are days yet!" he shouted. "Days!"

He laughed, the sound like a series of coughs, something wrenched out of diseased lungs. He raised his pistol and fired it three times into the air.

"Time," he yelled. "Plenty. Plenty of time. You can't avoid it. Days, yet. You will not hide!"

In his tossing boat, port-bound after taking up the morning nets, Duncan McLeod stood up, stared towards Lachan.

"Wisht, now, Gordon," he said. "That is the shooting again."

Gordon McLeod, his brother, turned round from his place on the small hatch. He said, "Aye, there are people on Lachan."

"I took them myself," Duncan agreed. "But they had no guns that I saw."

"There are rabbits, perhaps. They will want to hunt them."

"I told them there were rabbits. But I doubt there are many." He frowned. "And I saw no gun."

"Did you go through their packs and their packets, then?" Gordon asked, turning away.

"I did not. But a gun is no small thing to hide away."

"No. But it can be taken apart."

"Aye," Duncan agreed, if dubiously.

"Well, did they seem like murderers about their business, the day you brought them to Lachan?"

"No. But no man's a murderer by choice or profession. And there were two men and a woman."

"And one of the men foreign, as you say."

"Aye."

"And so you think there must be a killing at the end of it, then?"

"There were shots."

Gordon swung round again, stared at him for a long moment. "Aye," he said. "There were. And it's a great pity you spend so much time with the old folk watching that television and turning into a gowk as addled as the rest. Now we have fish to sell and no market to sell them in if we stay out here arguing about a pop-gun on Lachan!"

Duncan McLeod sighed, "Aye, you're right," he muttered. He revved the engine and settled once more to the monotony of steering the boat home.

Hassan had walked swiftly back to his cottage. His behaviour since seeing Martin had frightened him. He had been running to and fro like a two-year-old in a tantrum. But he was a killer, after all, trained in the systems of assassination. Twice he had been out-skirmished because he had forgotten that there were two of them, because he had let himself be distracted from one quarry by the appearance of the other. Now, although shaken by the fury which had carried him along like flotsam in a flood, he was determined to be rational, to plan.

"I have to catch them together," he muttered to himself.

Nodding, he searched among the suitcases. In a moment, he had found what he was looking for—the Ordnance Survey map he had bought, which showed the mainland and the cluster of off-shore islands. He laid a piece of writing paper on the table, took out his pen, began painstakingly to copy the outlines of Lachan.

He was totally absorbed in this. It may be that he was happy. His momentary dismay had been because of his loss of control; he had long stopped questioning himself about the rights and wrongs of what he was doing. That he should kill these two people now seemed so self-evidently right that the idea of a morality that would deny this or a normality that would consider it unthinkable were both beyond him. The situation had engulfed him. Like a child, or an animal, he was incapable of stepping outside it, of taking an objective look at it and in some way defining it. He merely acted now, responding to the twists and turns of time and chance, his role so totally accepted that he was no longer in any way aware of it. He would kill Ricky and Martin and this was an ordinary ambition, a straightforward problem. Only the question of how it was to be done presented itself to him. If he had been told he was mad, he would not have understood the word. He would have pointed at the map, neatly set out with its peaks and capes on the paper before him and asked if that could be the work of a madman. And if it had been put to him that the violence he was offering was an insane over-response to his situation, he would have replied, frowning in a puzzled way over his interlocutor's inability to think clearly, "But she rejected me. She ran away from me. How else will I punish her if I do not kill her? She has turned her back on me — of course she must be done away with, she must vanish. How can she behave like that and live?"

For Hassan had now absorbed his world. Like some enormous suction pump, his mind had taken in the universe. Everything that existed was no more than an extension of himself. He might simply have wished Ricky and Martin dead and so destroyed them in that world, and later, if there was to be a later, he might reach that stage; in the meantime, still tied to the remembered facts of a physical universe he had, in the reality of his myth, already incorporated, he tried to kill them — on the basis of the self-evident proposition that whoever denied him and thus the world must be dead already.

As Hassan, with his new, methodical fanaticism, squared off his map of Lachan, Martin and Ricky sat in the lip of their cave.

Martin said, "There's no sign of him."

"You could see?"

"From The Peak? Of course — it's bare on those slopes. And look at the view from here."

From where they were sitting, they could see over a mile of the southern shore to their left, nearly as far along the western cliffs. It was almost noon; the sea birds that had flung themselves in scattered skeins across the cliff-top air the whole morning were settling now. Ahead of them, about fifteen miles into the haze, they could see the indistinct shape of Coll. To the west, the sea lazily rose and sank under the gold-white sun. Around them, unseen insects hummed about their commerce.

"Christ, it's so peaceful. It doesn't seem possible that . . ." Martin shrugged, unable to describe the feeling of dread he carried, his awareness of the sinister reality that Lachan, despite its colours and its brightness, had become.

"This morning was a bit disastrous," Ricky said softly.

Martin shrugged. "A draw. We tried to trap him, he tried to trap us."

"But he was reading our minds; we weren't reading his."

"It's not only that—he's got a weapon. If we could produce something . . . It would put us a jump ahead of him, too."

"I suppose you've got an automatic under your arm. Don't tell me—your name was never Martin Prescott, you're actually Vladimir Illyich Prochovni, and Hassan is a KGB agent come to assassinate you. No wonder you weren't getting anywhere as an architect."

Martin laughed, a little thinly. "I don't know about not getting anywhere being an architect got us here, and now look at us."

"In any case, they never trained you in weapon design, so I suppose we'll just have to throw stones."

"Should have spent more time at the darts board, in that case."

He picked up a stone, flung it at a passing gull. With an undulation of one wing, it swept out of range as the stone passed far beneath it.

"Good shot," Ricky remarked. "In that time, Hassan could have let off a dozen bullets."

"What we want . . . "Martin began, then abruptly stopped. He bent, absent-mindedly picked up and threw another stone. Then he swung round, said, "Take your pants off."

Ricky stared at him. "What?"

"Yes, yes." Martin laughed. "I've become a pervert: undies-mad. I want to mutilate your knickers. Off with them!"

Ricky hesitated a moment, then slowly stood up. "Look here," she said. "This is a small island. It's too small for one madman, but two really won't leave much room for the rest of us."

"Off with them!"

She shrugged, warily lifted her skirt. Martin momentarily diverted from his first enthusiasm, suddenly fell on both knees, kissed her on the inside of her right thigh.

"Beautiful," he said. "I wish I could live there."

He stood up again, nodded. She stood for a moment, her eyebrows high. Then, without another word, she took off her pants, handed them to Martin. He nodded. He took the knife from the floor of the cave, made a little nick in the fabric, pulled the elastic from the waist.

"Knicker-mutilation; you were right," Ricky remarked.

"Not so—weapon-design."

Martin doubled the elastic, stretching it, let it snap back.

"If it did for Goliath . . ." he murmured.

"Catapult?"

"As approved by the modern schoolboy. All we need now . . ."

"In the meantime, I suppose, I'm supposed to get a cold on the bladder."

"You can pin them," Martin said, throwing her pants back.

"Thanks. Find me a pin," she replied. But he had gone, running along the cliff-top path, past the broken ground that lay beside the cave, the knife in one hand and the elastic in the other. In about ten minutes he came back, proudly carrying a Y-shaped piece of wood about eight inches high.

"We're in the armaments business, mistress," he said.

He nicked the top of each arm of the Y, pulled one end of the elastic through the first of these, then fastened it with knots. Next, he cut a small square of cloth out of one of the blankets, made two small slits in it and threaded the elastic through them. He put the end of the elastic through the nick on the second arm of the Y, twisted it round and round until it was firm, then threaded it once more through the cloth and so brought it back to the first arm of wood, where he secured it as tightly as he could.

"Double strength," he said. "You see? Silent, vicious, tested on a million greenhouse windows."

"Let's see if it works," Ricky said drily. "If I'm to go around with droopy drawers, I want to know it's been worth while."

Martin picked up a stone, fitted it to the square of cloth, braced his right arm, pulled the elastic back with his left, the cloth and the stone pinched in that hand's fingers. He took a deep breath, and let go. There was a faint hum, then the diminishing throb of the stone. It flew straight and true, out over the cliffs and rocks, to drop in the sea a hundred yards away. He sat down very slowly.

"It works," he said, in a high voice, his expression one of the utmost astonishment.

"Didn't you think it would?"

"No. Not really. I just wanted to see your legs again." He smiled, not looking at her, then leaped to his feet. "Now I'll have to practise," he cried. "I used to be quite good when I was a kid. I need marks, stones . . . a bit of time . . ."

"I'll keep watch," Ricky said, and got to her feet. She kissed him, picked up the knife, then began to scramble up towards their look-out point below The Peak. Below her, Martin picked out a mark fifty yards away, began to send stones whistling across the afternoon.

When, three hours later, she came back down again to report that she had seen nothing, he showed her how proficient he had become.

"But you'll have to learn," he said. "If you have to look after yourself . . ."

She took the catapult, stretched elastic, watched the flat parabola of the flying stone. "It's beautiful," she said. "In the light—like a comet!"

Martin nodded, climbed to the look-out three hundred feet above. To his right The Peak itself bulged against the sky. Between sparse bushes he could see the glint of the stream a mile or more away. To his left, the low, bare hills stretched away towards the north. To the right of the stream, the ground fell away, bare but for clumps of fern and heather, occasional broom bright-yellow in the sunlight, and dark-green rowan. In the distance ran the low humps which, like petrified dunes, guarded the shore to the east. Behind him, seabirds called raucously. He lay, wishing for a cigarette, for a cup of coffee, for relief from fear, watching the empty island, the leaping shadows of the scattered clouds, listening to surf and wind.

Three miles away, Hassan moved cautiously between two low peaks. He searched a shallow cleft in an outcrop of rock, then glanced around him and nodded. Out of his pocket he took the map he had made and drew a line across it, from the outlet of the stream on the north-eastern shore across to the opposite coastline.

"A third," he said to himself, smiling. "A third searched and covered. There will be time."

He had looked thoroughly, had spent the whole day about the task. He had found no trace of Martin and Ricky, no sign of a place where they had slept or hidden the tins and blankets they had taken, no sign of tracks, of sudden movement; he could for the moment disregard this end of the island. He sat down, regarded with some intensity the rest of the map. There was a natural triangle made by the line he had drawn, the coast before him and the stream which bisected Lachan. That would be the next area to search. He glanced at the sky; there would be light enough for several hours yet. He rose, cautiously began his new round of exploration.

"Where do you think he is?"

"Building traps. Thinking. Maybe searching." Martin sounded almost uninterested in Hassan's whereabouts. He glanced left and right, happy that they had not yet been discovered.

Ricky had climbed up to join him, tired of having reached a stage of proficiency with the catapult in which she could dispatch a stone in the general direction of a target without having any confidence that she would actually hit it more than once in a hundred tries. Now she lay beside Martin, her elbows on the short grass, her chin in her palms, Lachan below.

"And when he finds us?"

"It depends how, it depends where, it depends who sees whom first."

Ricky glanced at him. "It's funny," she said. "Here I have to depend on you. I feel I must. I'm out of my depth; I don't understand the landmarks of this situation."

Martin looked slightly embarrassed. "I'm no commando," he said.

"No. It's not that. But I haven't the strength, the kind of mind . . . Don't you feel oddly . . . clear? As if all sorts of problems have been resolved? Inside you—and between us."

"Not resolved, perhaps; just superceded."

She shook her head. "No. There's been a sort of resolution. I'm terrified out of my wits and yet . . . I'm happy. Or at least I feel as if I have a place, as if I'd found something. I suppose it's pretty atavistic, and in a way I'm ashamed of it. But couldn't this be the way we were meant to live?"

"What? Cramped into a corner by the fear of death? Threatened by a homicidal maniac?"

She smiled, but refused to accept this definition. "No—but

fighting, watchful; surviving in the most direct way. And the two of us . . . I mean, man, woman—a basic unit, working together for protection . . . I don't want to be romantic about it, it's too real and too horrible. But I feel no . . . no shame here if I defer to you, if I give you a simple admiration or accept an order without question—it's right here, it's proper for the situation."

He looked at her, surprised at her seriousness and at the simplicity of her reactions. He had known her as complex too long.

"And I," he replied in a low voice. "I feel no hesitation in protecting you. I'm as terrified as you, but I'd die. It's really as clear as that. I'd die if I thought it would mean your getting clear. It becomes quite obvious that you're the precious thing in my universe. So you have to be saved. It's easy, a simple logic. All the other rubbish . . ."

"Ambition's not rubbish," she interrupted, but breathlessly.

"No, it's not; except out here. There's no room and no time for palaces or municipal centres or petrol stations. It's just life, just hanging on to life . . ."

He put his hand out, softly stroked her hair. She turned towards him and for a moment seemed as if about to cry. Then she bit her lip, nodded at the sky, murmured something about the evening. Martin sighed, knelt, looked all around.

"Look, I'll prepare the cave," he said. "You keep watch."

He kissed her on the cheek, quite softly but with an affection that pimpled her skin and put shivers down her back. Then he climbed down to their cave and the small platform before it. For a moment he stood there thoughtfully, considering its situation. About fifteen feet below him, the cliff-top path wound round the island's southern tip. It was about a foot wide, with the cliffs themselves below it and, above it, the steep slope in which the cave stood.

Inside the cave, he picked up a blanket, with the knife and his hands ripped off a piece about half an inch wide. He cut this in half, to make two strips twenty inches long. He made four more of the same size, then carried them down to the path. He spent the next hour collecting sticks, firm pieces of wood cut from the tossing cliff-top bushes, stunted, tough, more stone than vegetable.

He sharpened these, some only at one end, others at both. The sky was darkening into evening when he had finished and the seabirds were whirling in their evening parade.

He tied his strips of blanket to those of the short sticks that he had sharpened at one end. On either side of the path below the cave, at intervals of about eighteen inches, he made shallow holes. Then, with a heavy stone, he drove the short stakes firmly into place, leaving the strips of material stretched across the path about six inches off the ground. Pale brown, like the earth, in the dusk they were already almost invisible.

Between these, he drove in the slightly longer stakes he had sharpened at both ends. In this way he booby-trapped about four yards of the path. Anyone coming that way in the dark would have his problems with sharp sticks and trip-wires.

Finally, Martin pulled a long thread from the thin woollen jersey he wore. He anchored this on the cliff side of the path, by means of a large stone, then ran it across and up the slope, to fix it on a bent-back branch of broom growing from the clinging turf. On this he hung an empty tin; inside the tin, he placed a small stone. He smiled; he had his early warning system. No one could walk along the path without brushing the thread that crossed it. It would be enough to pull it from under its stone, the branch would fling back, the stone would rattle in the tin, giving out its cow-bell message of strangers.

He was in the process of putting the same sort of device up on the path that led north along the cliffs, when he heard Ricky calling him from the cave above.

"I thought you were down here doing the cave-work," she said.

"Decided to construct Festung Lachan instead."

"Some fortress—three walls and a cut-up blanket," she remarked bitterly.

"Women don't understand strategy," Martin replied calmly, tightening the last knot, then tapping his empty tin to make sure that the sound was in it.

"We could put up prayer-flags as well," Ricky suggested.

"Anything that helps," Martin agreed, scrambling up towards her.

They stood side by side in the entrance of the cave. To their left, the remnants of the summer sunset still scalded the edges of the sky.

"What will help?" she asked.

"Anything. Whatever we do. It's almost a . . . a moral problem—the only solution to it is not to give up, not to lie here waiting for him to find us and kill us if he can. We mustn't be fatalistic, whatever we do; we have to keep acting."

"But everything we do . . . it's so little, so ineffectual."

"We're still alive."

"We've had luck."

"We've invited it. We've put ourselves in the way of luck, by planning, by facing him, by not lying down . . . Oh, we could lose and all that stuff on the path is no more than Boy Scout rubbish—but it makes me feel better to have spent an hour or so on it. And feeling better is as good a psychological base from which to plan action as any I could think of; isn't it?"

"You feel better; I feel worse," she said, glumly. Martin laughed and pressed her closer to him, but she shook her head almost stubbornly, as though refusing comfort. "No, he's out there, skulking somewhere in the night, planning ambushes, murder . . . But it's not as definite as that. All this is misery . . ."

"That's not what you said this afternoon."

"No. But it's night now and I . . ." She began to cry, standing straight and keeping an inch of distance between them. "I'm afraid," she said. "If I could think of him as man, someone ordinary but bad, simply, evil in a way I could realise or accept . . . But he's mad. It's different. There's no way we can reach him, no way we can make contact. He's not in our universe at all. What could we say to him, how could we make ourselves . . . known, yes, known to him as human or real or? . . . I mean, he's all there is, for him; we're extensions of him because he's put us in his fantasies and I hate it. I hate it! It scares me. It's as if I weren't being allowed to be me. It's as if he were a sort of vampire, a spiritual vampire, taking the life out of my soul, out of who I am. Can't you understand that? And I hate it, it scares me, I'm afraid of it."

"You are Miss Erica Mead and I am Martin Prescott and I love you. Do you love me?"

"Yes." She nodded, looking away from him.

"Then you are Miss Erica Mead and I am Martin Prescott and

169

we love each other. You don't need him to give and take identity. For God's sake, you have me!"

She looked at the ground, suddenly almost smiling.

"Yes," she said. "It's just a sort of . . . nightmare. All I have to do is think about it. It was just . . ." She gestured at the night, at the sound of the unseen sea and the soft skeins of wind that crossed the darkness.

"Shall we eat?" he asked.

She nodded, then asked, "What's left?"

"Not much."

They set out the last of the ham, a few scraps of cheese, a third of the salami, half a loaf of dry bread. They had olives and a finger of milk to go with this, and they had in reserve the small tin of pâté.

"It we keep that for the morning," Martin said, "with a few scraps of bread, we ought to breakfast quite well."

"And then?"

"We go and forage," he said, smiling.

"God, without you . . . if you weren't here . . ." She came to him, pressed her forehead into his shoulder, then kissed him and sat down. They ate, hardly speaking now, suspended in a sort of fragile happiness. When they had finished, Martin laid out the blankets.

"I'll watch. Three hours, then I'll wake you."

"Three hour watches?"

"If that suits?"

"It's better than two hours, worse than four."

He shrugged. "Four's too long. You can get tired."

He watched as she snuggled into the blankets, pulled them over her shoulders.

"It's hard, this ground," she said. "Next time we rob him, we ought to get one of the air mattresses."

"I'll make a list before we go. Remind me."

He bent down, kissed her. His right hand stole under the blankets, spread over the warmth of her stomach, then moved up to squeeze her left breast. She drew a sharp breath, felt herself rise towards this caress as though suddenly magnetised.

"No," she said. "No," her voice urgent. "If that begins . . ."

He laughed. "You're superstitious. You think it's a sin and he'll catch us as retribution."

"I think we ought to keep a watch. That's practical. If I thought we were sinning I wouldn't have let you touch me in the first place."

"You touched me," he said.

"Well, I wouldn't have done that even more. Anyway, it was only a hand on your arm."

"The moment was tense. The gesture seemed significant."

"It was." She smiled. "We haven't ever talked about it."

He nodded. "Perhaps this is the time to remember beginnings."

She shivered suddenly. "Near the end?" she suggested.

He stood up, laughing. "Well, I meant nothing so fraught with the transcendental and the chances of mortality. Just what we were talking about this afternoon how all this effects us. Now get to sleep. I'll call you in three hours."

He watched as she pulled the blankets over her ears again, then went out into the cool night. He stood for a while in the cave entrance, trying to see the path below him and the small traps he had laid there for the one prowler who might happen along. Then he settled the catapult he had made more securely in the hip pocket where he carried it, ran the stones his left-hand pocket held through his bent fingers and, humming under his breath, climbed a few feet up the slope until he could stretch out above the entrance of the cave. Slowly his eyes grew accustomed to the night. He could see the steepness to left and right, not yet lit by the late, waning moon but most faintly aglow perhaps under starlight. A few clouds stained the blue-black sky, carried by a slow wind. Martin sighed, settled down to watch.

Elsewhere Hassan moved cautiously through darkness. He felt keyed up, buoyant beyond the possibility of fatigue. He searched, his head down as though, like a hound, he could sniff a trail. But he saw nothing but the bushes, the riven ground, the hollows between hills. To his right, The Peak bulged against the sky. In front of him, the stream brawled through the night.

A few hours later, while Ricky watched and Martin slept—she anxious, her eyes wide, measuring tussock and shadow; he sprawled in the sleep of the exhausted—Hassan had satisfied himself that north of the stream there was no one. He crossed the water at Upper Pool, began to cast through the hills that would lead him the two miles to the north-eastern shore.

The sky was beginning to lift and lighten as Hassan stepped out above the sea. His zig-zag course had brought him across no sign of Martin and Ricky. His eyes red-rimmed now, he looked up speculatively at the six-hundred-foot high bulk of The Peak. Slowly he sat down.

"The highest point," he muttered. "I wonder . . ."

He ran across broken ground. Ricky, naked, ran before him. He could see the swell and bounce of her buttocks as she leaped over the rocks and fissures of the land. A sun burnt down, whiter than above deserts. Ricky grew, a pale figure enormous, monstrous, striding endlessly away from him.

"Wait," he called. "Wait for me!"

He ran, waving his hands before him like a blind man. But the ground gave way, disappeared, and he fell, tumbling endlessly toward annihilation. He screamed, his mouth stretched wide, his eyes straining to observe the final recession of the sky . . .

With a start, he awoke. Sunlight glittered across the water and struck at him like blows. He was stretched across stone, his head twisted to the left. Slowly he got to his feet, but he felt dizzy, almost too weak to stand. He scrambled up the low bulge of land behind him, found a clump of broom; in its shelter he stretched out, allowed himself to be claimed by his dreams.

.   .

In London, Detective-Sergeant Harroway said, cryptically enough, "Dumfries."

Melton nodded, glancing at the map open on his desk. "Going westward. The coast? Maybe a jaunt to Eire—a private affair; friends, or a hired boat . . ."

Harroway looked down at the map, a little moodily.

Melton asked, "What did they take this time?"

"A Mini. Red Morris. Absolutely ordinary."

"Dumfries are quite sure?"

"Scoured the town after they found the Vauxhall. It's not a large place."

"When was the Mini taken?"

Harroway seemed almost embarrassed. "Anything up to three

days ago."

"Three days!"

"They wanted to be sure."

Melton stood up abruptly. "They may very well have made sure. Three days! Long enough for rigor mortis and a bit left over."

Harroway cleared his throat, said nothing.

"All right," Melton snapped. "Switch the search. West and north of Dumfries—concentrate there; no point in assuming they've changed direction. And we'd better get up there, so arrange it."

Harroway hurried out of the office. Melton sat down again. Aimlessly, his finger moved over the indented coast of Scotland.

.   .   .

When Martin came back to the cave after his second watch, he found Ricky sitting up.

"I'm thirsty," she said.

"I know. But we only had that milk. Now . . ."

"The stream's a mile away; not more. If we could fill one of the tins, at least . . ."

"I've used the tins to make my warning system. We'd both have to go down there, drink . . ."

"That bloody nonsense with bits of string!" she suddenly shouted. "Christ, you're really having a good time. I suppose not since the Cubs . . ."

She began to weep, bending low, so that her face was almost in the blankets that covered her legs. Martin stood above her, awkwardly bending to stroke her hair.

"I know," he said, not certain of what he should say. "I know."

"I was dreaming, that's all. That we were together somewhere —it was beach, holidays; everything was easy . . ."

"It'll happen," he said. "It'll be all right."

"Yes." She mopped at her face with a corner of the blanket. "I must look like the last of the tinkers. As for you . . ."

He grinned. "We're the highest society Lachan has to offer. We can set our own standards."

But he was worried by the spasms of hysteria she was beginning now and then to show. He laid out the last of bread, opened

173

the tin of pâté, cut the bread in slices, covered these with the meat, handed her one.

"No," she said. "Without drink . . ."

He ate, chewing slowly, trying to check the discomforts of thirst. Then he folded the blankets, put them against one sloping wall of the narrow cave.

"What do we do now?" she asked.

"We wait."

They watched the morning without speaking more than a few words. At about ten o'clock he climbed to the top of The Peak, lay there, watched the spread axe-shape of Lachan below him. Nothing moved on it. There was no sign of Hassan and he began to wonder if Hassan had left. But he knew that was more wish than likelihood.

Ricky climbed up to join him.

"I wish I thought it was beautiful," she said bitterly, nodding at the landscape. "I wish I thought it was more than an ambush."

"It'll revert," he said. "Give it time. We'll remake it."

"You haven't seen him?"

"He's down there," he assured her.

"Yes."

They lay side by side, their eyes darting towards every soft movement, every fluttering fledgling.

"I'm thirsty," she said. He glanced at her. Her lips were dry and parched, the skin flaking off them. She looked very pale. Her grey-green eyes seemed too wide, too brilliant.

"I'm thirsty, too," he said. "We'll drink as soon as it's dark."

Two miles to the east, Hassan stirred under the broom, twisted to his right, muttered about his dreams, then sank once more into silence.

"How many days are left?" Ricky asked.

"Five, before Duncan McLeod calls for us."

She shook her head. "It's too long. And even then . . ."

Martin glanced at her. "What then?"

"There's only one beach. If Hassan knows when McLeod's coming, he'll wait for him. If he'll kill us, why shouldn't he? . . ."

"We can't put other people into danger, that's true."

"What do we do, in that case?" The edge of hysteria was back in her voice. "How do we get ourselves off?"

"We'd have to signal, or get to McLeod first, or jump Hassan . . . There are days yet to think of that."

"Yes," she agreed bitterly. "Days."

Long clouds, spun out like threads, pulled across the sky. The wind rose slightly, kicking the sea into hissing movement. Guillemots and gulls yelled for their afternoon fish, then dipped under the wind to pick them up themselves. The sun, pale in the pale sky, dropped westward, until it lined the hills to the left of The Peak with a golden yellow.

Ricky said, "I'm thirsty."

Her voice was hard, scratchy; when she had spoken she swallowed convulsively twice. She rolled over on her back, blinked at the late afternoon.

She said, "I must have been asleep. Or hallucinated. I think I dreamed."

"What?" Martin drowsily asked.

"I don't know. It must be hours since we talked, but it seems just . . ." She shrugged, let the sentence drop. She shut her eyes and like a child, watched the patterns within her eyelids.

Martin glanced down the long sunlight. There was no sign of movement, no sign of Hassan. Where was he waiting? What trap had he prepared, what bait, coiled spring and final hook?

"God, I'm thirsty. Thirsty."

Ricky whispered this, not opening her eyes. Then she rolled over twice, her arms loose. She giggled softly, then turned on her stomach, buried her face. Martin imagined she was crying again, but had not the strength to offer comfort. He looked up at the sky. It would be bright for hours yet.

He said, "It'll soon be dark."

"But we've not seen him. All day—not a sign."

"Do you believe he's there?"

Ricky hesitated, then nodded. "Yes," she said dispiritedly, "he's there."

"Well, then, he's waiting. Biding his time."

"Our time."

"Yes. All of us waiting—we have to wait. Only the dark will help us."

But in the event they could not wait for full dark. Unused to privation, having drunk nothing for twenty-four hours, they allowed themselves to be seduced into movement as dusk swept sea and sky clear of the last contamination of sunlight. And elsewhere, Hassan, cold and stiff, awoke to find the day fled with his dreams and another night upon him.

Walking unsteadily round and round, rubbing his eyes, smacking his lips, he wondered at his waste of the light. Would he have the whole island to search again? What if the others had found him, asleep and vulnerable? Irritably, he stumbled across the shoulders of hills, making his way towards the sound of water. A wash, a drink, something to refresh; then food at the cottage—then the night to search in, the high places to investigate. Smiling, he walked on, already pulling his sleeves back from his wrists, anticipating the bite of the cold spring water.

"Where?" Ricky asked, her voice hushed. She peered left and right, as the gloom transformed bush and crevice into danger.

"The nearest water. We'll have to veer right. We'll want the western branch of the stream. But let's spread out a bit—if he is about it'll give him less to shoot at."

Thus, in open order, they walked cautiously across the long, bare shoulder of The Peak, until, hearing water in the distance, they began to hurry.

"God, it's awful," Ricky called.

"Shut up," was all that, grimly, Martin would reply.

In the cool of the gathering night, the stream sounded clear and inviting. In a moment, they could see it, flashing with the last of the light as it dropped over stone and pebble towards the junction with the eastern tributary and then Upper Pool and the bridge between the cottages and the sea.

Ricky began to run, her feet unsteady on the uneven ground, her arms waving like a dancer's. When the shot split the evening, it was this, perhaps, that saved her. Hassan, as before, had shot too eagerly. His attention and concentration divided, he had regretted in any case that he had pulled the trigger in the same instant as he had done so; thus unsighted and unnerved, he sent his bullet flying to the right of Ricky, as if at the last moment he had tried to pull his pistol over to threaten Martin instead.

"Down!" Martin yelled, dropping.

As he fell, he heard Hassan shoot again, twice; and then, in the distance, laughing. Martin, panting, listened dry-mouthed to the stream's seductive burbling. He glanced across at Ricky. In the semi-darkness, he could see her slowly, cautiously, mov-

176

ing backwards. To her left was heather in black clumps. She rolled towards this, disappeared. To keep her safe, Martin leaped to his feet, plunged to his right, then dropped again.

Flame scraped briefly at the dusk. Fern fronds shredded, scattering their primeval green over Martin's shoulders. He lay still, his head burrowing into the turf.

"Come and drink!" Hassan's voice was high, on the verge of laughter. "There is water here. Come and drink it!"

Martin glanced towards the spot where he had last seen Ricky move. She had gone, either moved off, away from the ambush into safety, or to ground in some way, hiding among roots and shadows, as he himself was.

Cautiously, he knelt, crouching like a sprinter.

"We have to drink," he shouted. "We must have something to drink."

"Come, then," Hassan's voice replied.

On the first word, Martin leaped forward, ran through the knee-high fern and heather. From the opposite bank, Hassan hesitated. He could see only the swift shadow, hidden against the bulk of the hills beyond, the nebulous marks of movement. Traversing with his pistol, he breathed deeply, then shot. From the far side of the stream there was a shout, the cessation of movement, a threshing a moment later among invisible plants; then Martin's voice, muttering in a tone almost tearful. This was followed by a groan, another—then silence.

Hassan waited, testing the other's pain or patience. But nothing more moved, no voice sounded, demanding help or revenge. Hassan let ten minutes pass, then fifteen. Finally, very cautiously, he stood up.

Elsewhere, Ricky, her breath like a scream in her throat, ran along the stream. Upper Pool was behind her. In a moment she would see the dark oblong of Hassan's cottage. There would be water there, in the green plastic canister that stood beside the door. Hassan would have filled it; he was careful, provident, domesticated. But mad, she remembered. Then she would fill it, she cried to herself in silent fury. If it was empty she would take it to the stream and fill it and carry it back to Martin . . . to Martin . . .

But she would not think of Martin, or of the gunfire that had sounded behind her; nor of the silence that had followed it. There! That was the cottage, the shape of the cottage. She swung to the right, her eyes already intent for booty.

Hassan, cautiously jubilant, stepped slowly on a flat stone that bisected the stream. As he straightened, something flew, humming, past his head. An insect, swift and late? He hesitated, momentarily startled. A new hum, a buzzing; then an abrupt splash beside him.

"Stones!" he shouted, laughing. "Throwing stones!"

He leaped forward, running up the slight rise which led from the stream, straining towards the place where he had seen Martin fall. But Martin stood, suddenly twenty yards to the left, his right arm bent back, his left stretched. Hassan, swinging round, heard the hiss of elastic, ducked as he shot and knew he had missed.

He screamed, his teeth clenched with fury, his whole face, his whole being, convulsed with frustration. The whole of his will was concentrated on killing this organism that defied him, that had refused to accept that in the universe he had invented, which he carried in the infinity of his mind, he himself was the sole dispenser of power.

"You are dead!" he shouted. "You are dead, dead . . ." and ran parallel with the stream, his feet thrusting through the stiffness of the heather. Martin moved quickly to the right and Hassan, running, tried a snap-shot. But his foot turned on an unevenness, his bullet flung into the night.

Hassan dropped, lay still. Warily, he waited. Let Martin take up the initiative of movement.

Long minutes dragged by. The small plants moved as the wind crossed them. The wind? Or? . . . Hassan rolled, crouched, waited. No, it was the wind. He smiled, half-snarling; was he afraid that the stalked would turn hunter? He watched the darkness, waited for Martin to move. The surf, a mile away and then all around at greater and greater distances, fell and soughed and whispered. If he could clearly hear, disentangle the new sounds, the out-of-place rustles from those that might be here at any time, on any evening . . . Frowning, he concentrated; the night remained without revelation.

Martin, then, had gone. Yet he and Ricky had been thirsty. Would they give up water so easily? But there was water elsewhere, another branch to the stream. They would surely have

178

moved backwards, hidden in the night, crept away, slaked their demanding thirst. He was in wait for no one.

"Come back!" he yelled suddenly. He stood up, unsteady in his anger. "You thief! You whore! Yes, and the whore! I have heard you . . . But I shall . . ."

The stone bit, hissing, through the night. Hassan heard it and moved, not able to see it in the split second of its flight, turned his head, bending to his left; so that the stone, half an inch across and travelling at eighty miles an hour, caught him flush on the cheekbone and with one short cry of pain he fell backwards. He put his hand to the cut, feeling the warmth of blood. Fifty yards away, the doubled shape of Martin was running now, stretching away and out of sight. He fired, watching Martin drop sideways, then, dimmer now, get to his feet again and run off into the shadows.

"You bastard!" Hassan shouted, shooting again and again. "You bastard! You are dead! Oh, believe me, you are dead, dead!" But the night hemmed him in, set him apart, made him solitary, a hunter deprived of his prey. He put his hand on his cheekbone, set off at a run for his lair. He could not see, half a mile to the north, the straining figure of Ricky, hurrying back to the cave with her captured water container. Even when he was at the cottage once more, he did not notice the canister's disappearance; instead, marching to and fro in a fury he thought his flesh and bones would not withstand, he screamed his threats at the cloud-littered, star-broken sky.

Martin crossed Ricky's path a little ahead of her. He had been prepared to cast back to the stream to search for her; now, hearing someone clattering through the brush and broom, he huddled against a cascade of granite, his muscles tense, his catapult poised in his left hand.

When he stepped out of this ambush she screamed, then, recognising him, set the canister down and ran to him.

"All that shooting," she cried. "Oh, I'm so glad you . . . And you aren't hurt? No? Nothing? I was so frightened. So scared."

Hugging her, "But you disappeared," he said. "You just sank into the ground. I didn't know . . . I couldn't think . . ."

She laughed excitedly. "I took his water. I took his water-tank. That plastic . . . I thought that we'd need . . . that if we were to get thirsty again . . . No, to creep down like this

179

time and find that he . . . No, I couldn't do that again."

"You took it!" Astonished, he laughed with her, then, carrying the water in one hand and holding her to him with the other, he walked her over The Peak's shoulder and down to their cave, telling her the story of his catapult's triumph.

At the cave, she took bread and some drying cheese from her pockets and they ate this, these few crumbs she had stolen, enough to make them realise how hungry they were without doing much to satisfy; then she curled as always into the blankets and he climbed above the cave's entrance to take his usual watch.

But it was Ricky who, four and a half hours later, sat staring on the hillside, straining to hear once more the soft scrape of — what? — on stone. A footstep? Landslide? Searching animal? Searching what? Who searching?

Moving an inch at a time she slid towards the cave's entrance. There she hesitated, listening again. And once more a soft scraping, an instant's carelessness, perhaps, out in the hunting dark.

"Martin," she whispered. She leaned back, pressed his shoulder.

With a gasp he awoke, rolled to one side as though afraid. As if this had been a signal, fifteen feet below, the warning tin suddenly let loose its rattle. A man's voice shouted. Martin threw off his blankets, came to his feet; in the same movement, he picked up the catapult that had been lying beside him.

The man's voice — Hassan's voice — rose to them again; there was a thud, followed by a scratching sound.

"He's fallen," Martin said.

He moved cautiously out of the cave, slowly and as silently as he could climbed down towards the path. He stared into the darkness, but other than the occasional white curl of a wave two hundred feet below, he could see nothing. Hidden in the darkness, Hassan lay, stretched at the edge of the drop, his left hand searching for his fallen pistol. If Martin could have seen him, taken his chance, jumped those last dangerous feet in two long strides, to settle like some preying bird on the anxiously hunched shoulders . . . But Hassan's fingers found steel, curled about the ribbed butt. He rolled from the cliff-edge, knelt, looking wide-eyed about him. From the hillside a stone rolled, then flung out into silence. Hassan fired at the sound, twice. Out of the darkness came the hum of a catapulted stone. At the same time a cascade of small rocks descended from above; Ricky, at the cave mouth, was taking a hand.

"You are found!" Hassan shouted, firing again and again. The scream of ricochets laced the darkness with danger. "You are trapped!"

Martin, spread-eagled on the hillside, waited a moment, then let fly again, aiming for the flashes that kicked in split-seconds of brilliance from the pistol's muzzle. Hassan turned from the stone; he could wait, now, he could watch, blockade; kill in his own time.

"Oh, you are found now, you are dead now. You have no chance; only death."

Laughing, he turned, ran back along the path. In the light he would return. Behind him, Martin reached the path, began moving after Hassan.

"Martin!" Ricky called.

He stopped, hesitated. "What is it?"

Breathlessly she said, "You . . . you mustn't follow him. If you follow him . . . It's what he'd want you to do. We must be together . . ."

In the darkness, Martin could hear Hassan laugh, then call out, "Wait! You wait there. In the morning . . ." The syllables seemed long, like a ghost's wailing. Martin turned, climbed back to the cave.

For a long moment he and Ricky embraced, not having words with which to discuss their fear. Then Martin laughed, the sound sharp, nervous.

He said, "The alarm system worked, in any case."

She shrugged. "For him too."

"Yes. Now he's certain we're here. But he'd have found this place in any case. At least now we know he's coming."

"We ought to move. If we could go out along the cliff path . . ."

"No. He'll be above us. It's moonlight from now on. If he sees us against the water . . ."

She glanced out. The sea was bright with the yellow light of the new-risen, waning moon.

"Above us? Do you think? . . ."

"I heard him climb. He's no fool. He's mad, but still thinking, operating on his delusions. If he sits somewhere near the top of The Peak, he can look in both directions. He'd see us as soon as we moved, almost. And be able to pick us off."

"Then what?"

"He'll come from above us tomorrow. Otherwise we'd see him. And I've as much chance of hitting him at the distance from here to the path as he has of hitting me."

"You can't kill him."

"I can hurt him. But we've got to trap him, in some way . . . At any rate, get him to commit himself. Look, there's that hollow, isn't there? All that broken ground above the path north. If we could find a hole there . . ."

"I want distance," she said. "Otherwise, what's the point? That hollow's only a hundred yards away. If he doesn't find us here, he'll be over there in five minutes. For five minutes it isn't . . ."

But Martin was not listening. "We have to commit him," he said. "He has to make a move first. Then at least there's a chance. If we sit still in this trap, he makes his move and we've nowhere to go. Check-mate. If we go too far, he sees us. Check-mate again. To the south there isn't anything—it's hole up those few yards to the north, or suicide."

She shook her head, then shrugged. "I don't understand the rules of the game. You and Hassan . . . or perhaps it's just men . . ."

They picked up the blankets and, moving very cautiously, aching at their vulnerability, they crossed the open slope to where outcrops of rock marked the beginning of the riven ground where Martin hoped to find hiding and, with luck, his counter-ambush. They found a sharp-edged declivity, round and ragged as a crater, and settled in it, huddled close together, their breathing swift, their eyes wide and anxious, waiting for the dangers of dawn.

Eleven miles away, Gordon McLeod said angrily, "And soon it'll be fairies. Any knocking in the night at all. Our business is with fish."

Duncan McLeod said levelly, "If we have no concern for people, perhaps we should be under the ocean with the herring."

"But a banging—it might have been anything . . ."

"It was shooting and we both heard it and we both knew it.

Now you may stay out here and fish, but the boat and I are going back."

"But what policeman will listen to us?"

"You don't think Macrae will take me seriously?"

"Well, Macrae . . . But if it turns out to be some sort of dream. A delusion, maybe, and the folk are laughing at us for a couple of gowks . . ."

"Rather that," Duncan McLeod said placidly, keeping his course dead-straight, "than be pointed out as murderers by default."

The dawn was easy, peaceful, pale, then brightening, with not an angry mark of scarlet in the sky.

Martin said, "Now," in a sort of grim, last-fling determination, and set himself to watch. Ricky sat below him, hidden by the rim of their hollow. Sometimes she made swift, nervous gestures, picking at her hair or rubbing her hands together; at other times she sat very still, leaning back against the uneven rock as if in rehearsal for death. The sun, hidden from them for the first part of the morning by the bulk of The Peak, at last appeared above it. The heather hummed with insects. The day was mockingly beautiful.

And nothing moved in it.

"What's he waiting for?" Ricky asked, over and over.

"Us," Martin told her. He felt cunning, sharp; yet fatalistically prepared for whatever might happen to them. "Time plays on his side—as far as he's concerned, we're sitting in the cave, remember. Cooped up there, we'd be wondering what he was up to behind us, above us. Sooner or later—and he's got days yet— sooner or later we'd be bound to come out, explore, separate . . . He wants us in the open."

"Even here," she said. "Even here. I can't stand it much longer."

Across the water, two uniformed policemen stepped boisterously into the McLeods' boat.

"If you've just been hearing things, Duncan," one of them began.

"We're not a family with the sight, Macrae," Duncan McLeod replied. He whipped the motor into life, pointed the bows towards Lachan. "In any case, you telephoned, you'll have your orders now. And a man can't make a mistake when he has his orders."

Gordon McLeod said, with a bitter loyalty, "Och, there was a noise all right. A sort of popping, a sort of distant . . . Well, it was shooting. Yes, yes, it was guns all right."

"Mermaids, perhaps," the other policeman said.

"Then one half would be your concern," Duncan McLeod retorted, "and the other half we'd take to market."

"And that car now," Gordon said, "that had some meaning for you. What was the importance of the car, Macrae?"

But the policeman did not answer. As the boat lifted on the long swell of the deeper channel, the four men settled for the journey.

It was noon when Ricky said, "We forgot the water."

"Let it lie then," Martin answered, irritable as his tired eyes took in, over and over again, the details of this bare landscape.

"But I'm thirsty," she said. "I'm thirsty again."

She fretted in this way, off and on, for over an hour. Martin tried to ignore her, but worried, hearing the note of hysteria edging back in her voice. And Hassan remained invisible, hidden somewhere in the hazy, lazy, sea-framed day.

"I must drink," Ricky announced, with a sudden firmness at half past one. "I must drink something."

"No. We've got to stay put."

"I have to drink. He's not there. He's not out there. You can see, you can tell . . ."

"I'm sorry." He watched the familiar horizons flicker in the heat. "You'll have to stay here."

Ricky stood up, not bothering to hide. Her face was very pale, her expression harsh, twisting her mouth into an almost cruel grimace. Her eyes seemed very large and bright.

"It's just a little way. You know he's not out there. I have to drink something. I can fetch that container back here."

"He's waiting. Can't you understand that? He's waiting for a movement, for a noise, for your head to appear on his horizon. Just as we . . ."

"Well, I'm going."

She climbed without another word over the side of the hollow, began to walk quietly towards the cave.

"He'll kill you!" he called, jumping up to follow her. She began to run and he hesitated. It was near; a minute or so would see her journey over. If Hassan found them together he would kill them both; if he saw only Ricky, he might refrain. Ricky he wanted, not as corpse but as sexual partner. And now it was too late to stop her, anyway. If Hassan was watching he would already have seen her. And would let her go, Martin knew, because it would be in his interest; he would want to know the precise location of their hiding-place.

On the other hand, if she died, if the sound of Hassan's pistol gathered the afternoon into some final, destructive moment, how would he himself ever be able to continue living?

"By killing him," he muttered. And he knew that if Ricky were murdered, there were no extremes of strength and cunning he would not be able to reach in his need to balance Hassan's death against hers.

He stood, with expressionless face, letting these thoughts and a thousand other fears and intuitions race through his mind. His body seemed stiff and bruised when he once more became aware of it. He felt the pain in his eyes as he stared again and again at the half circle that faced him.

The minutes went by. Minutes? How many? In a sudden panic, he looked at his watch. But he did not know when Ricky had gone, at what time she had left him. Surely she had been away five minutes at least? Perhaps more! Wildly he examined once more the line of hills to the left, the rise and curve of The Peak in front of him, the sharp bends of the cliff-top path to the right. Nothing moved. No one had shot or shouted. Everything looked untouched, peaceful; empty.

He glanced at his watch again. It was four minutes since he had looked at it first. Nearly ten minutes had gone by, then, since . . . Was she simply taking that drink of water? Or—her manner had been so strange, so distraught—had she forgotten what she had gone for, was she walking on, perhaps humming to herself as she walked, stooping to pick the occasional wild flowers, her danger expelled from her mind? He moved agitatedly to and fro about the hollow, he craned his neck, he listened with sudden total intensity.

Ricky sat, white-faced, in the cave. Three feet from her was the green plastic canister, still a quarter-full of water. Beside it, Hassan stood, a gentle, distant smile on his face, a Buddha's smile, an expression of total dissociation from the world.

"He will come. Then you will see," he said. "He will come. Then you will understand. It is a question of power. I want you to see this; because if you understand it, perhaps you will be saved. It is what I ask, not more—a small amount of understanding. That is enough, understanding is enough; out of it, other feelings will grow. If you truly understand, that will be inevitable."

The voice went softly on, the eyes, their darkness paradoxically bright in the gloom of the cave, looked past her into the light beyond. The lips moved, but the round face was without expression. He sounded like someone repeating lines too-long rehearsed, or like a robot programmed to make this speech over and over again.

"Ricky!"

Martin's desperate voice, long past caution, called from a little way away. She moved, half-turned; Hassan pushed his pistol higher, nearer.

"No sound, yet. Otherwise, all the chances are over."

She stared at the gun, feeling tears suddenly in her eyes; but whether they were for fear or anger she had no means of knowing certainly. She sat without a word.

"Ricky!"

Martin, nearer now, traversed the steep slope. Below him the sea hissed lazily against rocks, then ran back in cascades of a hundred thousand points of light. His eyes, bloodshot from fatigue, rolled in his head as he searched the sunlit hillside. But he saw nothing, heard nothing.

"Ricky!" he shouted and then, with a sort of catch of fury in his voice, "Hassan!"

Hassan's smile broadened a little. Almost sleepily he nodded at Ricky.

Ricky called, "I am in the cave."

Martin heard the voice trickle down to him from the cave-mouth, which was fifteen feet away and about five feet higher up the slope.

But what had been wrong with the way she had spoken? The tone had been right; yet there had been something unnatural, a formality about it, something stilled . . .

"What?" he asked, shouting.

"You know that I am in the cave," she called back.

All the words spoken! Every syllable clear. That was it. Like . . .

"I am coming!" he called back.

Yes, like Hassan. Hassan, who spoke his student's super-perfect English, in which nothing was ever slurred, in which "do not" never became "don't"; Hassan, who might never notice in someone else's speech something so habitual in his own — Hassan was in the cave with her, had asked her to speak, to play bait to his trap and call Martin to death.

Martin climbed slowly. He moved automatically, like a som-nambulist. It was as though the day had come to a stop, time suspended; or had in some way lost substance, so that at any moment one would see through the insubstantiality of matter to an endless grey Sahara beyond. All light receded, sunshine, wave-glitter, beauty—Martin in his new isolation moved to-wards the cave-mouth.

When he was level with it, when it gaped silently beside him, he stopped. He closed his eyes. He did not know what to do, what action was possible to him. He rubbed his forehead like someone dazed.

"Are you there?" he called.

Even as he spoke he knew he had made a mistake, pinpointed himself for Hassan's sudden bullets. Without thinking he flung himself forward, leaping across the cave's opening, to land and slip, then steady himself, on the far side.

Hassan swung as Martin jumped; but too late. The bullet sang out over the dappled sea. He and Ricky could hear Martin's shoes slide, then hold, on the steep slope to the left of the entrance.

"Well?" Hassan demanded. "After all . . ."

He leaned forward, hit Ricky with the back of his left hand, the movement sharp, too swift to avoid. She fell sideways, the marks of his knuckles high on her cheek.

"No," she said in a low voice. "No."

Hassan bent over her, grabbed her wrist, flipped her over so that she lay on her stomach. He put his pistol in his trouser pocket—elsewhere, Martin pondered frontal attack, then knew it useless—and, with cord that he had carried for the climbs that might await him, he bound her wrists together, then pulled her ankles high and attached them to her fastened wrists. He pulled a scarf between her teeth and bound it tightly at the back of her head. Slowly, he stood up, looked down at her. He smiled. He took out his pistol, pointed it at her, smiled again as she shut her eyes convulsively. He bent and with his left hand gently stroked her buttocks, uncovered by the wrenching-back of her legs. Then he sighed, stepped carefully towards daylight.

Martin, who had scrambled higher up the steep hillside, lay across the ground's unevenness, staring down towards the cave. Where was Hassan? Would he come out? Where was he? Waiting? For how long? And Ricky, Ricky—was she safe? What was Hassan doing? When would he come out? Would he come out? And if he did? . . .

Hassan, looking left, crept into sight. Martin could see the gleam of sunlight on the barrel of the pistol he carried. Hassan hesitated, craning his neck to look round the bulge of the hill-side. Martin, twenty-five feet higher, panting through parched, wide-open lips, slowly crouched, then knelt.

Hassan swung round, looked to his right. Martin steadied his catapult, squinting to take aim. He pulled steadily at the elastic. Hassan looked up.

For a second it seemed as if they would speak; they stared into each other's eyes, strangers in total communication. Then Hassan flicked forward his right arm, fired. Martin, late in releasing his stone from its sling, watched it fly wide. At the same moment, he realised he was lying, was rolling, then wedged. Only then did he feel the punch he had received in his shoulder, the sudden thrust of metal and velocity . . .

"Hit," he muttered. "The bastard actually . . ."

He heard, through gathering ripples of pain, the slide of a shoe on stone and shallow scree. He stood, bending double for cover, ran to his right. Here the hillside curved away. He would be out of sight, out of reach of the bullets, of Hassan's eye.

A half-mile away Duncan McLeod said, "There's another one."

Macrae, the policeman, nodded sharply. "Proves nothing. They might be practising, simply; having fun."

"Aye, they might. But then you'd best go and see if they have a licence for their gun, Macrae. It's just your duty."

Gordon McLeod said, "Oh, they're deep, the police—when you saw their little car it was telephoning you were before anything else at all could happen. But now it's all coolness and good sense. Might you not know these people on Lachan, Macrae?"

Macrae did not smile. "I might," he agreed.

"And did we not then have to wait for your friend here in case your strength should not be sufficient?"

"Yes," Macrae said, grimly. "So now we'd better hurry, McLeod." And he stared tight-jawed at the approaching, tilted shape of the island.

Martin scraped and slid down the hillside. Somewhere to his left and above him, Hassan crouched, waited a moment, then ran—to find Martin gone from the place where he had seen him fall.

Martin, level with the cave, swung across towards it. In a moment he was at the entrance. Ricky lay, trussed in the shadow. Martin raised his eyebrows interrogatively and she nodded reassurance. He ran on, once more climbed the slope to the left of the cave. He reached the shallow rift where he had fallen, crouched in that scanty shelter. A stone slid by him, bound helter-skelter for the cliff. Above him, Hassan, casting to his left, searching for the beast he had wounded, came briefly into sight. Martin stood up, tugged at his catapult. Hassan, hearing it snap, turned, his pistol flashing. But the humming stone caught him on the neck. For a moment he dropped to his knees, choking.

"Dead," he coughed. "You are dead now."

Martin was in the open, a sacrifice willingly offered. Controlling his breathing, Hassan got to his feet. He set the smile on his face again. He walked to the edge of a long outcrop of granite, as if he might preach from this high pulpit; thus exposed, he seemed to scorn Martin's ridiculous schoolboy weapon. He raised his pistol, watching Martin's frantic heaving at elastic, the anxious wavering of the catapult in his hand. Now there would be no deviation from destiny; time had run out. The hunt was almost over.

Round the hillside, walking easily along the clifftop path, came two uniformed policemen.

Hassan stood, unable to move or speak. His eyes dilated; he felt as if he would vomit. He blinked; there could be no one there. But the blue uniforms stood, pink faces stared up at him, one of the men pointed.

Martin, below, saw nothing—only Hassan, poised on his rock like a vulture. He knew he could not beat a pistol, knew that stone against lead bullets was prehistory outmatched; he knew that he was on the verge of death. He let the sling go, watched the stone lift like a bird. Hassan half-moved his head, seemed to make some gesture with his left hand, a sort of movement of denial. The stone hit him on the temple. For a moment he staggered, his wide-flung arm sawed across the sky. Then, screaming, he toppled. In a dark blur he fell past Martin. Arms and legs sprawled as if for jokes, he hit scree, then grass. For a moment he dragged over loose soil, seeming safe; but the hillside dropped sheer and he was free again. He hit the narrow path, his left shoulder first. For a second or more he seemed balanced like that, a vaudeville act taken beyond spectator's rights. Then his legs turned in a slow cartwheel and with a sort of snarl, the last voice of his despairing madness, he dropped over that two-hundred-foot sill into the waiting death below. And, falling, conscious, felt beyond terror a last snapping of tensions, a sudden ease, hearing himself scream, stretching for hope, believing that in the end . . .

.   .   .

On the mainland beach twelve miles away, Detective-Superintendent Melton climbed out of a car, glanced at his watch.

"No launch?"

"It's ordered," Harroway soothed.

"But late."

Side by side, the two policemen looked out towards the distant shelf of Lachan.

Behind them, the uniformed driver said, "It's the nearest point, sir."

"We know." Harroway did not turn round.

"A sort of desert islet," Melton murmured. "We should have guessed."

"There are hundreds, sir."

"Then we should have searched them."

Harroway made a small grimace. "At least some of the local police have already gone out there."

"After the shooting's begun, Harroway. What sort of timing's that? Shooting, perhaps people killed—what's been our role, what's our responsibility?"

"We do our job, sir. We don't have a lot of options open to us."

"If people have died, then we chose the wrong options."

The two men glanced at each other, then back out to sea.

．　　　．　　　．

On Lachan, under The Peak, in the now-redundant cave, "Where is he?" Ricky asked, then choked, half smiled, and choked again.

"Fallen," Martin said. He undid the last of the knots that had held her. His face was grey; he moved very slowly. His voice sounded dull, beaten toneless.

"Fallen?"

"Yes. He fell. I hit him with . . ." He stared at the catapult beside him; then, almost petulantly, he picked it up and threw it from the cave. "He was high up," he went on. "On the edge of . . . Anyway, my stone hit him, it hit him; and he fell, on and on, he shouted, falling . . . Anyway, he fell."

"He's dead?"

"Yes. Dead. As easy as that. It can happen to . . . Just a stone, you know. It hit him and . . ."

"You're wounded," she said.

Ignoring this, he asked her, "How did he? . . . I mean, where was he hiding? I didn't hear you . . ."

"In here. He knew. That we'd wait, then, sometime, we'd come back. He was just sitting here, waiting. It was easy once he'd caught me—you were bound to come. I was so afraid. But I thought—people often don't know what they sound like. And you understood!"

"Yes." Martin nodded, leaning forward so that he seemed on the verge of sleep.

"It's finished, then?" Ricky asked.

"Over. Yes. There are some men . . . I saw some men on the path. Policemen, I think."

"Policemen!"

"So perhaps I needn't have actually . . . But I didn't see them. I hadn't seen them when I let that stone go. I just didn't know they were there. But he'd seen them. Must have. And stopped, you see—didn't move. And I . . . Christ, death's too easy. We shouldn't have that kind of strength. It shouldn't have been made as simple as that."

He bent towards her, kissed her, then kissed her again more strongly.

"Yes," he murmured. "Yes, that takes the taste of it away. Yes, that's life and summer—it's not gone. It's not gone, after all!"

He smiled suddenly, pulled her more tightly to him. "And there were lessons learned," he went on. "That's something. And you're here—and summer; it's all still living. That moment's gone by; we're still here. And will be—oh, for summers yet."

On the island's small beach, Melton and Harroway clambered from their launch. Their efforts already futile, made pointless by events, they hurried sweating across pebbles.

But behind Martin, Macrae, a shadow against the afternoon, asked politely, "Would it be possible for you to tell me what is happening on Lachan?"

Martin laughed abruptly, the sound dry and soprano, as if he were a little mad.

"Yes," he said. "We're having the beginning of an engagement party. Everybody's invited and we intend that it should last for forty years."

Then he lay back, laughing in great uncontrollable bursts until he finally fainted from the pain in his shoulder.